'Laura, I'm  in what you...

'If you have an... them to me. Yo... things on your... eyes on her, his g... over the oval of her face in such an intent fashion that she felt her cheeks flush with heat. 'You're a good doctor, and you should have confidence in yourself.'

Nick laid a hand lightly on her shoulder and turned her towards the doctors' lounge. 'Now, go and get yourself some coffee.'

Laura didn't know what to think. She wasn't used to having him quite so close, and it was becoming increasingly difficult for her to concentrate when his arm was draped around her like that. It was a totally innocuous gesture, but the warmth of his hand permeated the thin cotton top that she was wearing, and his gentle touch was doing unbelievably strange things to her insides.

A&E DRAMA

Blood pressure is high and pulses are racing in these fast-paced, dramatic stories from Mills & Boon® Medical Romance™. They'll move a mountain to save a life in an emergency, be they A&E doctors, nurses or paramedics. There are lots of critical engagements amongst the high tensions and emotional passions in these exciting stories of lives and loves at risk!

A&E DRAMA

Hearts are racing!

Recent titles by Joanna Neil:

A CONSULTANT'S SPECIAL CARE
EMERGENCY AT VALLEY HOSPITAL
HER CONSULTANT BOSS
THE CHILDREN'S DOCTOR

THE DOCTOR'S FAMILY SECRET

BY
JOANNA NEIL

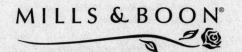

MILLS & BOON and MILLS & BOON with the Rose Device are registered trademarks of the publisher.

First published in Great Britain 2003
Harlequin Mills & Boon Limited,
Eton House, 18-24 Paradise Road, Richmond, Surrey TW9 1SR

© Joanna Neil 2003

ISBN 0 263 83880 3

Set in Times Roman 10½ on 12 pt.
03-0204-50751

Printed and bound in Spain
by Litografía Rosés, S.A., Barcelona

CHAPTER ONE

'WE SHOULDN'T have to wait for too much longer before we can get an X-ray picture of your leg, Lewis,' Laura said gently, trying to encourage the fretful five-year-old in her care.

He wasn't at all happy because of his sore limb, but at least she had done what she could to make sure that he was reasonably comfortable in the wheelchair.

'I'm sorry that they're not ready for us yet. Tell you what, we'll go and have a look at some of the pictures in the corridor, shall we? It will help pass the time and I think you'll like them.'

'All right.'

Laura turned the chair and pushed it carefully into the corridor outside the X-ray department. At the far end of the passageway, a man came through the swing doors.

He was walking purposefully in their direction and she cast him a quick glance as she manoeuvred the chair into position. He was tall, dressed in an immaculately tailored suit, the jacket loose to reveal a pristine shirt, and as he came closer, her heart sank in quick recognition.

Nick Hilliard was the last person she'd expected to see, but it looked as though even down here there was to be no escaping him. The specialist registrar managed to get everywhere, didn't he? Sometimes she couldn't help wondering if he followed her around deliberately, just to annoy her.

Reaching them, he stopped to give her a quick nod.

'Hello, Laura.' Nick's deep voice was rich and smooth, rippling over her senses like dark melted chocolate. Why did he always have that effect on her? It put her at a disadvantage, when she would much rather keep a clear head.

Nick turned his attention to the child. 'Hi, Lewis,' he said, his smiling glance travelling over the little boy. 'Are you all finished here and ready to go back to A and E?'

Lewis shook his head miserably. He squirmed in his seat, but couldn't move very far because his left leg was stretched out in front of him, supported by a padded footrest. 'They're not ready for me yet.'

'They're not?' Nick's blue-grey eyes darkened in a frown. 'You've been down here for quite a while, haven't you?'

Lewis nodded. 'I was getting fed up, so Dr Brett brought me out here to look at the pictures in the corridor while we wait.'

'I see.' Nick turned his gaze on Laura, and she stiffened a little, tightening her grip on the wheelchair.

'It's only been a few minutes really,' she murmured. 'It just seems longer, that's all.' She looked around for something that would distract Lewis.

There was a beautiful appliquéd tapestry decorating the wall in front of them, and she moved the chair so that he would be able to see it properly. Perhaps the colourful scene would take his mind off things for a moment. The poor boy had enough to put up with, suffering pain and discomfort, without having to wait around in total boredom.

Nick followed her movements, his gaze narrowing on her as she reached over to set the brake. The stretchy cotton top that she was wearing rode up with the movement of her arm, and suddenly she worried that it might be just a little too clingy. Her skirt, too, was a snug fit, hugging the curve of her hips like a warm caress. She had raided her wardrobe this morning, searching for clothes that would be comfortable and easy to wear, but right now she was beginning to doubt the wisdom of her choice.

To her relief, though, Nick turned his attention back to Lewis.

'Mum's gone to phone my dad and tell him what's happening,' the child confided.

'That's a good idea,' Nick said. 'At least he'll know that you're all right, and in good hands.'

The boy shifted restlessly in his seat. 'Mum says I might have to stay here for a few days.' He chewed disconsolately at his bottom lip. His fair hair gleamed under the overhead lights and Laura noted that his cheeks were faintly flushed with fever. His leg was obviously distressing him, and the reddened, swollen area around his shinbone was plain to see. Understandably, he was feeling uncomfortable and out of sorts.

Nick gave him a thoughtful look. 'I know this is upsetting for you, Lewis, but we'll get you sorted out as soon as we can. In the meantime, I'm sure that Dr Brett will look after you, and your mother told me that she's going to stay close by, so there's nothing for you to worry about.'

Reaching into his jacket pocket, he drew out a small plastic box wrapped in Cellophane and then crouched down beside the boy so that he was at his level. As he leaned towards the child, Laura found herself staring down at the faintly bronzed nape of Nick's neck. Her glance strayed. His black hair was attractively styled, cut short in clean lines, and rays of sunshine slanted in through the window behind him, picking out iridescent lights.

'Here you are,' he said, softly, handing the box to the child. 'You can have this, if you like.'

'What is it?' Lewis looked curiously at the small package.

'It's a kind of puzzle,' Nick explained. 'You fit the pieces together in different ways to make lots of funny-looking people. If you're feeling up to it, you might want to play with it for a while.'

Lewis's eyes widened. 'Thanks.' Intrigued, he pulled at the wrapping, then opened the box and began to sort through the cards that were in there, his mouth gradually quirking into a smile.

Watching the boy, Laura's mouth softened. She had seen Nick do this kind of thing before, and she had to admit that he was very good with children. He had a way of putting them at ease, and she guessed that he must have a store of small games and puzzles that he produced to distract children whenever they had to sit and wait for a diagnosis or treatment.

Seeing that Lewis was preoccupied, Nick straightened up. He looked at Laura and frowned, drawing her to one side. 'What's going on here?' he demanded, his voice low and terse.

'I thought it best if I brought Lewis down to X-Ray myself.' The mass of her bright curls tumbled around her face, lightly brushing her shoulders in its usual un-ruly fashion. In a defensive gesture, she pushed back a coppery strand of hair from her cheek. 'We aren't too busy in A and E at the moment, and I was due for a break. He seems more settled with me around, so I thought I would bring him here and then go and grab some lunch.'

'I realise all that, but you came down here ages ago.'

Laura shrugged lightly. 'That's a matter of opinion. Anyway, the radiologist had just begun to take a series of X-rays of a rheumatoid patient from one of the afternoon clinics, when we arrived. It's taking longer than we expected.'

'It certainly is…much too long. We have critically ill patients in our department who need to be dealt with as quickly as possible.'

'It's hardly the radiologist's fault,' Laura pointed out mildly. 'I'm sure she's working as quickly as she's able.'

'I appreciate that,' Nick said firmly. 'What I'm saying is that it's not right that our patients should have to wait at all. I've been saying for a long time now that we need an X-ray machine dedicated for A and E use.'

'If it had been an outright emergency I would have intervened, of course. As it is, I expect we'll only have to wait for a few more minutes and then Lewis can go in.' Laura's finely arched brows drew together. 'You're probably asking for too much if you're expecting the department to get new equipment at the drop of a hat. You and I both know that funding will only stretch so far.'

His jaw tightened. 'So your father says. I'm sure that if he put his mind to it he could bring his influence to bear. And it isn't just the question of the X-ray machine—it's the whole set-up in A and E, especially where children are concerned. It's a soulless place for them to have to wait to be treated. There's no atmosphere whatsoever, just dull, plain hospital surroundings. It's enough to put any child off.' He was glowering now. 'Something needs to be done about it.'

Laura held back a faint sigh. They were back to this again, were they? She had only worked at the hospital for around three months, and in all that time she and Nick had hardly ever been able to see eye to eye on things, especially where her father was concerned.

A faint atmosphere of antagonism had sprung up between them almost from the beginning. At first she had put it down to the fact that she had been brought in to replace another doctor who had been scheduled to start work on the team. A domestic upheaval had caused the man to change his plans at the last minute and move to another area instead, and from all accounts Nick had been put out by that turn of events. He had been part of the initial interview panel, but the way things had gone, it must have seemed as though Laura had been foisted on him, and she had been a completely unknown entity.

Now, though, Laura wondered if the real thorn in Nick's side was the fact that her father was chief administrator here at the hospital.

'My father does what he can. He doesn't make the decisions on his own…you know that. He has to consult with the rest of the management team.'

'I also know that he holds a lot of sway with them and, if he wanted to badly enough, he could change things.' He glanced down at his watch. 'I have to get back to A and E right now, but I'll have a word with him later on today. There are quite a few things I need to go over with him.'

The determined set of his mouth alarmed her. 'I don't think that's a very good idea,' she said hurriedly. 'Not just at the moment. This is his first day back at work, and he'll have a lot on his plate…' But Nick had already turned away and was moving swiftly along the corridor.

She would have called after him, but at that moment

the radiologist appeared and beckoned her into the X-ray unit.

'Sorry to have kept you waiting,' the woman said. 'Do you want to come through?'

'Thanks.' Laura gave Lewis a bright smile. 'Come on, then,' she said. 'Let's have a look at what's going on with your leg, shall we? As soon as we have the pictures we can decide what needs to be done to make you feel better.'

She already had some idea of what the X-rays might reveal. Lewis's mother had brought the child into A and E, and she had explained that her son had been limping for the last week or so. Gradually, his condition had worsened, and now the limb was severely painful and it was also beginning to suppurate at the point of tenderness, although the mother was fairly sure that Lewis hadn't banged his leg or hurt it in some way.

She had also mentioned that Lewis had been quite ill with a chest infection, and Laura believed there might be some connection.

The X-rays took a few minutes, and when they were done, Laura wheeled the little boy back along the corridor.

'We'll go and meet your mother in A and E,' she told him. 'Why don't you have another look at your puzzles while we're on our way? They're fun, aren't they?'

'OK.' He nodded tiredly and winced as he tried to move his leg into a more comfortable position.

Laura felt a surge of compassion for the little boy. He reminded her so much of her young nephew, although Connor was a year younger than Lewis. They both had the same mischievous features, despite the fact that Lewis's were tinged with pain right now. She couldn't imagine how she would feel if Connor was ill.

The sooner she could start Lewis's treatment, the better. She had the X-rays, now all she needed were the results of the blood tests she had ordered.

Arriving at the A and E department, she pushed Lewis's wheelchair towards a cubicle that had been set aside for paediatric patients.

Lewis looked around at the austere white-painted walls, and his eyes were wide and frightened as he stared at the lifesaving equipment nearby, but he didn't say a word, and that worried Laura. There were no other children being treated right now, and she guessed that he must be feeling very lonely. She desperately wanted to comfort him.

'I'll draw the curtains around so that you can be a little more private,' she told him gently. 'I expect your mother will be here soon. Try not to worry, Lewis. We'll look after you, I promise.' She glanced at the box of puzzles in his lap and pointed a finger at a picture he had made up. 'Goodness, it looks as though that girl's had a real fright, doesn't it? Her hair's standing on end.'

'I bet she's seen a spider.' Lewis giggled. 'I'm going to make another one, with a really scary face.'

Laura smiled at him. 'I can see you're good at this.'

'I take it you've finally finished with the X-ray department?' A familiar deep voice came behind her and she made a faint grimace. Didn't that just prove what she had been thinking earlier? Nick seemed to follow her everywhere. He had scarcely given her time to settle her young patient before he had appeared once more.

'Yes, we've finished.'

'What was the result?'

Laura glanced down at Lewis and saw that he was still engrossed with his puzzles. At least they were taking his mind off his troubles.

'I need to check with the laboratory to be absolutely certain,' she said in a low voice, 'but I think the X-rays confirm that the original respiratory infection has travelled and is affecting the bone.' She turned to the nurse who had come to stand alongside the bed. 'Would you stay with Lewis for a while, please, Jenny? His mother should be back at any moment.'

The dark-haired nurse smiled. 'Of course.' She walked over to Lewis's side, and said cheerfully, 'I'm just going to make sure that you're comfortable, sweetheart, and then I'll take your temperature again.'

Laura moved out of the cubicle and drew the curtains behind her. Nick followed. 'So you think it's osteomyelitis?' he queried.

'I do.'

'OK. If you're right, you should admit him and start antibiotics. He may need surgical drainage.'

'Yes, I know. I'd intended to start him on antibiotics straight away.' Her green eyes flashed momentarily. Didn't he believe that she was capable of making her own diagnosis? Why did he feel it necessary to step in with advice?

She pulled in a deep breath. There was no point in feeling resentful, was there? After all, he was in charge while the consultant was away, and he was just doing his job as he saw fit. Maybe when he got to know her better he would come to realise that she was a good doctor, and that she knew her stuff.

Frowning, he said, 'You may find that you need to explain it carefully to the parents. They could be worried that it might mean a long spell in hospital for him.'

'It doesn't necessarily mean that, though, does it? He might have to take antibiotics for several weeks but, provided he shows signs of improvement after his initial stay in hospital, he could probably continue those at home.'

'Yes, you're right. Have you thought about analgesia?'

'Of course. It's obvious that he's in pain.' She sent him a brooding look. 'I am capable of looking after my patients, you know.'

His eyes crinkled at the corners. 'Sorry. It gets to be a habit, overseeing junior doctors. A lot of them are nervous when they sta ɩ work in A and E. They come across things they've never seen before, and they need as much support as we can give them.'

His unaccustomed humility came as a surprise, and she found herself looking at him in a new light. Her gaze travelled over his strongly sculpted features, the edges softened now by wry amusement. He was a good-looking man by any standards, but when he smiled it lit up his face, and she was uncomfortably aware of his sheer maleness. She looked away. She didn't want to find him attractive—that was the last thing on earth she wanted.

'I appreciate that you don't know me very well yet,' she murmured. 'But you can have confidence in me. I'm not going to let you down.'

'Well, we'll see. You wouldn't be the first to believe that you have it all under control.' He paused, and then added, 'There is just one other thing that you might not have thought about. It's possible that the parents might be feeling guilty. Perhaps that's something you should address.'

'Why should they feel guilty? They've done nothing wrong.'

'Sometimes parents feel that they should have recognised the problem before it reached this stage. That's something you might need to reassure them about.'

He walked away then, leaving Laura to dwell on his words. Was he right? Lewis's mother had seemed confident enough on the surface, though now she came to think about it, the woman had been a little weepy. Laura had put that down to natural worry about her son, but there could be more to it after all.

She went off to check with the lab about the blood tests, and just as she put the phone down, Lewis's mother came hurrying towards her.

'I'm sorry I've been away for so long,' she said breathlessly. 'I had trouble getting through to my husband at work. I didn't realise he was already on his way here.' She looked anxiously at Laura. 'How is Lewis? Have you had any results yet? Do you know what's wrong with him?'

Laura nodded. 'It looks as though Lewis's recent chest infection could be the source of his troubles. The infection has been carried in his bloodstream and is affecting the bone in his leg. It's a very painful condition, but we're giving him something to ease that.'

Mrs Watkins looked panic-stricken. 'It's bad, isn't it?' Her face crumpled. 'It's all my fault. I didn't realise how bad it was. I should have done something sooner.'

Laura shook her head. 'You haven't done anything wrong, Mrs Watkins. You must believe that.'

She grimaced inwardly. Much as it troubled her to admit it, it looked as though Nick had been right. The woman did blame herself, and it should be a lesson to Laura that she took too much for granted. She still had a lot to learn.

'Lewis had treatment for his chest infection,' Laura

explained, 'but the bacteria were aggressive and resistant. There was nothing you could have done about that.'

She gave the woman a reassuring smile. 'We're going to give Lewis much stronger antibiotics than those that he had before,' she said. 'We'll be giving them intravenously so that we can do everything in our power to beat this infection. We're expecting him to recover completely, but it will take a while, possibly a few weeks.'

'Will he have to stay in hospital?'

Laura nodded. 'Yes. Just for a week or so, until we're sure that he's on the mend. After that, as soon as he's well enough he should be able to go on with the drug therapy at home.'

'Can I see him?'

'Yes, of course you can. You can stay with him as much as you like. I'm going to set up his intravenous line right now if you want come with me.' Looking closely at the anxious woman, she added reassuringly, 'We'll soon have him feeling better.'

'Thank you. I know that you're doing all you can for him. It's just that he's so young…he's all that I have.'

'I'm confident that we've caught this in time,' Laura said softly. 'Come and see him. You'll be able to cheer him up.'

Laura was kept busy for the rest of the afternoon, and thankfully managed to keep out of Nick's way. She didn't want him breathing down her neck, watching her every move. It wasn't as though he singled her out for attention—he kept firm control over everything that went on in A and E—but she found his presence unnerving. It was bad enough that he hadn't wanted her on his team, and his ongoing disagreements with her father were an additional irritation.

She wondered how her father was coping. He hadn't

been well, and she had been concerned about him all day. Now that things had quietened down again, she could go and see him.

His office was on the next floor and, approaching it, she saw his door begin to open. She slowed her pace a little. If her father was at his desk, and free, she would pop her head round the door and say hello.

Instead, she heard the sound of a voice clipped in anger, and her heart sank.

'No, David, I don't see your point at all,' Nick was saying. 'In fact, you can take it from me that this is just the tip of the iceberg. There's a lot that can be done to make the department run more smoothly and efficiently, and I've a number of ideas as to how we can make the place more user friendly. I don't accept that it can't be done, and if I were in charge of the department I would be on your case every day. As it is, I'll make sure Tom Edwards knows what I think.'

Laura drew in a sharp breath. It was a good thing that the general public didn't use this corridor. It wouldn't have been helpful for them to hear the argument that was going on. She hesitated, not wanting to eavesdrop but not knowing what she should do. She had come to talk to her father, and it looked as though his meeting with Nick was about to come to an end. There was hardly any point in retracing her steps.

'I'm sure that Tom already knows what needs to be done,' her father responded shortly. 'As the consultant in charge, I imagine that he wants to see changes every bit as much as you do.'

He paused. 'Look, Nick, I do agree with you that we need to run the department in an effective manner. I know how important these things are, and what you're saying is reasonable enough, but it's a question of priorities. A lot of the time the X-ray machine that we have is left idle—evenings and weekends, for instance, when the outpatient departments are closed. Surely you must see that?'

'What I see is that patients are vulnerable,' Nick said firmly.

Laura stepped away from the door and began to examine the scene from the nearby window, but she could still hear what was being said.

'I don't think you appreciate the problems we have to deal with, Nick.' Her father's tone was curt. 'I'm made to account for hospital expenditure the whole time. We're overstretched as it is, and we have to make careful decisions as to what can be put in place.'

'That isn't my concern. My priority is the well-being of the patients.'

'Even so, you should be aware of the wider picture. Just keeping up with maintenance can be a minefield. Take the MRI machine as an example…it's a hugely expensive piece of equipment to maintain, and we're already paying people to man it for extra hours. There's a long waiting list of people needing MRI scans. Whenever the machine breaks down we have to get it fixed and back in action as a matter of urgency, or even more patients would be left vulnerable. We have to weigh one thing against another, and make decisions accordingly.'

'I know that, but you still need to take note of what I'm saying. I work in A and E almost every day, and I know what needs to be done to make the department function better. I want management to know exactly what we need to make this place second to none.'

'Believe me, you've made your position very clear.' Laura could imagine her father's tight-lipped expression.

'I can assure you that I will put your ideas to management.'

'I'm glad to hear it, but I won't hold my breath waiting for anything to happen,' Nick said, thrusting the door open even wider. 'And much as I'd like to stay and argue the point with you, I have an A and E department to attend to.'

David's comment was equally terse. 'And I have a desk full of paperwork and a lot of catching up to do. I'll talk to you later, Nick.'

Nick swept out into the corridor and slowed to a halt as he saw Laura. She pretended to be engrossed in the view of the landscaped quadrangle below the window, but she glanced up as he approached.

'Is my father free now?'

He sent her a seething glance. 'He's all yours.'

'Well, that's good. I thought I would spend my coffee-break with him.' Without further ado, she walked into the office and closed the door behind her. After the exchange she had just heard, she didn't care that she'd left Nick standing in the corridor.

'Laura…it's good to see you.' Her father looked up and put aside the file that he had just opened, laying it down on the desk.

'How has your first day back at work gone? I've been worried about you. I didn't think you were well enough to come back yet.'

He shook his head. 'It was just a virus. I'm well enough now and, anyway, I get bored just sitting at home with nothing to do. I may just as well be here and getting on with things.'

Laura looked at the paperwork cluttering his desk. 'You mean you wanted to get back to work because you knew all this would be piling up. You work too hard.

I'm sure that's why you got the virus in the first place. They put too much on you.'

She studied him carefully. 'I just saw Nick coming out of your office. Has he given you more problems to deal with?'

He gave a faint grimace. 'I expect that young man will go far. I always knew that he would be a man to be reckoned with one day. When I was a consultant here, he was on my team, and I could see that he was energetic and full of ideas. He has a quick intelligence, a brilliant mind, but he's also headstrong and impatient.'

'He's giving you trouble?'

'He wants to see things change, and he wants it brought about quickly. So do I, but I'm used to the way these things work. Nothing gets done overnight, no matter how hard you push. It's the way things are, and I've learned not to let it get me down. There are people in management who have their own ideas of what changes need to be made, and everything is a matter of compromise.'

'Are you regretting that you went into management?'

'No, not at all. I couldn't carry on as an A and E consultant after the accident affected the use of my hand, but I knew that I could be an effective administrator and that my experience as a doctor would be invaluable in making sure that administrative decisions were solidly based.'

Laura reached out and covered his hand with hers. 'And now you have Nick hassling you every day. That wasn't what you'd bargained for, was it?'

He smiled wearily. 'It's all part and parcel of the job, I suppose. I need to try to meet Nick halfway because he's full of good ideas, and basically I've always thought that should be encouraged. I think we might lose him otherwise, and much as we rub each other up the wrong way, and as much as his going would make my job easier, it would be a great loss for the hospital, I'm sure. There aren't many men who have his expertise.'

Laura frowned. 'Is that a possibility? Is he thinking of leaving?'

'I know that he wants a post as a consultant. He has all the qualifications necessary and I know that he's been looking around.'

If Nick went, that would make things easier all round, Laura reflected, but she kept her thoughts to herself. The way things were, the constant arguments with Nick couldn't be doing her father any good at all. 'I wish there was something that I could do to make life easier for you. I hate to see you looking so drained.'

He smiled. 'If I look like that it's only because I've been unwell for a while. Anyway, you do enough to help me already. It's good to be able to talk things through with you. I know you have a difficult job of your own. I know what it's like to deal with the cut and thrust of A and E. It isn't easy.'

'Which reminds me,' she said, taking a quick glance at her watch, 'it's time I was getting back to work.' She gave him a quick hug. 'I'll see you at home later.'

Back in the department, she checked on Lewis and then made the final arrangements for him to be admitted to a ward. His analgesics were working, and he looked a lot more comfortable.

She dealt with a few minor injuries, and was thankful that no major emergencies cropped up in the moments before her shift finished for the day. She had been on the go for several hours, and she would be glad to get back home.

Her jacket was in the doctors' lounge, and when she

went to retrieve it, she found that Nick was there, helping himself to coffee from the espresso machine.

He was frowning over the rim of his cup.

She glanced at him. 'You look serious. Is that because of a problem in A and E, or could it be that you didn't get what you wanted from my father when you went to see him this afternoon?'

'A and E doesn't give me too much of a headache. As for your father, at least now we both know where we stand.'

'I tried to warn you to stay away from him. I don't think you should be pressurising him right now. He's been off sick with a nasty virus, and this is his first day back in his office. I'm not convinced that he's fully well yet and, added to that, he has a backlog of work to get through. The last thing he needs is you harassing him. You need to give him time to get himself sorted.'

'If he's not well enough, he shouldn't be back at work.'

Laura glared at him. 'And then things really would grind to a halt, wouldn't they?' She pressed her lips together. 'I might have known you'd take that attitude. I don't think you appreciate just how much he does for this hospital. But, then, you've never tried to see things from his point of view, have you? If you did, perhaps you wouldn't be so hard on him.'

His expression was cool. 'Do you really think your father needs you to rush to his defence? I know that you came to Wales to be near him, and that you're living under his roof, but does that mean you have to watch over him every minute of the day like a mother hen?'

Her mouth tightened. 'That isn't what I do. I don't think you can have any idea of normal family life,' she said, fighting to keep her self-control, 'or you wouldn't talk like that.'

'I believe my family gets along very well together,' he commented mildly. 'We live within a reasonable distance of one another and we visit regularly. I was simply saying that the fact that you've been away from home for some time and only recently returned to the nest might have made you a little over-protective.'

Her head lifted. 'Since you brought the matter up, I'll tell you how it is. I moved back into my old home because it was the sensible thing to do. I needed somewhere to stay, and my father offered me a place. He and I get along well together and I care very much for him. But perhaps you find that too difficult to understand?'

Nick gave a wry smile. 'I understand it well enough. I just don't know what could have possessed you to up sticks and come back here when you had a perfectly good job in Lincolnshire. You were doing well at the hospital from what I heard, and you could have gone on to better things. The city had a lot to offer—good accommodation, plenty of nightlife. Why leave all that behind to come and live here in the wilds?'

'You seem happy enough to stay here,' she retorted. 'Why should I be any different?'

'I was born here. I grew up with the mountains all around, and the sound of the sea in my ears.'

'Perhaps you don't realise that I've spent most of my life here, too,' she said tautly. 'I went away to train as a doctor, to see what life was like in other parts of the country, but deep down I feel that I belong here more than anywhere else. And after my mother died a few years ago that feeling was even stronger. I felt that I needed to be with my father.'

She sent him a stony look. 'Seeing what he has to put

up with, I'm more than glad that I did return. I don't know why you have to be at loggerheads with him all the time. You shouldn't be pressurising him this way.' She pulled in a deep breath. 'Anyway, you're not the consultant in charge. Why don't you leave it to Mr Edwards to make the decisions? It's not right that you should go over his head. You'll be able to put your own ideas into place well enough when you're a consultant yourself.'

'You know as well as I do that Tom Edwards is near retirement. In the meantime, he's content to let things meander on in the same old way that they've always done. Besides that, it seems to me that he's not been well for a long time now. He won't admit it, but it all adds to him not wanting to alter the status quo.'

He had a point, certainly. Laura had noticed that Tom Edwards had been struggling to cope recently. It had been worrying her for some time because she knew that Tom suffered from angina, but he was insistent that he could cope and that he wasn't a danger to his patients. Up to now he had been managing, keeping his condition under control with medication, but she had a feeling that his attacks were becoming more frequent these days.

'At least you seem able to recognise frailty in some people,' she retorted. 'I was beginning to wonder if that was possible. I wouldn't put it past you to have his job in your sights already.'

Nick's expression was drily amused. 'You wouldn't be too happy about that, would you?'

'Not if it meant that you would have the opportunity to hassle my father even more than you do now. I think I would sooner you applied your energies to anything but that.'

'I'll do what I can to oblige,' he murmured, 'but I'm making no promises, you understand.'

She stared at him. There was a dancing light in his eyes that belied his words, and she sensed that he enjoyed riling her.

Turning away, she shrugged into her jacket. She wasn't going to spend time dwelling on what he said.

Even so, as she left the room the image of his wry smile stayed with her.

CHAPTER TWO

'ISN'T that your brother in the waiting room, Laura?' Sarah Harris, the triage nurse, surveyed the rows of patients who were waiting to be seen. 'Shall I send him along to see you?'

Laura quickly signed off a patient's chart and went to look through the treatment-room door to the waiting room beyond.

'Matthew...here? What on earth can have happened?' Worriedly, she noticed that four-year-old Connor was with him. 'I hope nothing's happened to Connor.' She filed away the chart and said quietly, 'It's all right, Sarah, I'll go and have a word with him.'

Connor must have seen her already, because he came rushing towards her with a whoop of joy. 'Aunty Lor,' he exclaimed, putting his arms up and hugging her around her legs. 'My daddy's cut himself. Can you make him better?' He looked up at her, his little face a mixture of enthusiasm and confident expectation.

'I promise I'll do my best, sweetheart,' she said. 'Let's go and talk to him, shall we?' Lightly ruffling his fair hair, she held his hand and walked back with him towards her brother.

'Hello, Matthew,' she said with a slight frown. 'What are you doing here? What happened?'

Matthew gave her a quick smile. 'It's nothing to worry about, really. It was just one of those stupid accidents. I wanted to have a go at fixing the fence back home, and I was cutting through a fence panel when it happened.'

He lowered his voice, turning his head away slightly so that his son wouldn't hear. 'I didn't realise that Connor was right behind me, and when he said something to me, the saw slipped and cut my hand. I don't think it's too bad, but I thought perhaps it might need a stitch or two.' His mouth made a rueful quirk. 'Catherine's out on a shopping trip, so I had to bring Connor with me. I wouldn't normally want him to be hanging around an emergency room.'

'Don't worry, we'll look after him.' She inspected Matthew's injured hand and winced. 'Come on through to the treatment room, and I'll take a proper look at it.'

Nick was already at work in the treatment room, and as Laura walked in he emerged from a cubicle where he had been examining a woman with an injured hip.

He spoke quietly to the nurse, asking for various tests to be carried out and calling for a surgical consultation. Then he walked towards Laura and said, 'Tom's dealing with a burns patient, and I think he might need someone standing by. Would you be able to do that?'

It was an unusual request, and Laura paused before answering. He hadn't asked her to assist, just to stand by. 'How urgent is it?' she queried. 'I can help, but this is my brother and his son, Connor. I'd like to attend to them myself, if possible.'

He nodded, glancing at dark-haired Matthew and the boy. 'OK. I'll get someone else to work with Tom.'

Laura frowned, sensing that there was something more going on than she was being told. 'Is there a problem?'

He gave Matthew and Connor a fleeting glance, and then said in a low voice, 'Probably not. It's just a feeling. Tom was looking a bit off colour this morning.'

'This probably won't take me too long,' Laura said. 'Matthew's had a bit of a disagreement with a saw. From the look of things, that hand will need three or four stitches.'

Connor fidgeted. He was looking around, his eyes screwed up in a frown as he took everything in. The unit was busy this morning. Several of the cubicles were occupied, and there was a smell of antiseptic about the place, which added to the austerity of the atmosphere. Laura had the feeling that her young nephew felt uncomfortable amongst all these strangers, who were all so much larger than him.

Nick must have sensed it, too, because he smiled at Connor and said, 'Perhaps one of the nurses can find you a colouring book and some pencils, or maybe a jigsaw. Would you like that?'

Connor nodded solemnly, but still clung to Laura's hand. He wasn't going anywhere. He was staying firmly by her side.

'I'll see what I can do,' Nick promised. Looking at Matthew, he studied his features carefully, and then said in a contemplative tone, 'I can't say that I can see much of a likeness between you and your sister.'

His blue-grey eyes travelled over Laura, coming to rest on her wild shoulder-length curls with a curiosity that made Laura's cheeks flush with heat. Her hair was naturally curly, and she had never been able to make it do what she wanted.

'Then again,' he murmured, 'perhaps you're glad that you don't have her flame-coloured hair.'

Matthew smiled wryly. 'That's true enough. It looks good on Laura, though. People say much the same about Connor and me because he's fair and I'm dark. He takes after his mother.'

Laura interrupted gently. 'I really think we should see to your hand now, Matthew, don't you? It must be very sore. We should at least get you cleaned up.'

Nick moved away to attend to his own patients, and Laura led Matthew to a cubicle, making sure that Connor was seated where he wouldn't be able to follow proceedings too closely.

After a moment or two a young nurse put her head round the screen and brought the jigsaws and colouring materials Nick had promised. 'There you are, young man,' she said lightly. 'These should keep you occupied for a while.'

'Thanks, Amy,' Laura said. At least while Connor was busy she could concentrate better on Matthew's hand. The gash was quite deep and rough around the edges, but she cleaned it up and injected a local anaesthetic, before suturing the wound.

'You'll need to keep it clean,' she told him. 'I'm putting a dressing on it, but you might need to pop into the GP's surgery and get that changed after a day or so. The stitches can come out in about ten days. I'll do that for you at home, if you like.'

'Thanks, Laura. I'm glad that you were on duty today. I feel foolish enough about landing myself in this situation as it is. I'd sooner keep it in the family.'

She grinned at him. 'Perhaps this will teach you to be a bit more wary. I thought it was common knowledge that when you have a four-year-old around you need eyes in the back of your head.'

He laughed. 'Just wait till you've got one of your own.'

Laura gave him a crooked smile. That wasn't likely to happen any time in the near future, was it? Up to now she hadn't met anyone that she wanted to spend her life with, and even when she did meet a man who was half-way decent, she always felt that some element was missing.

It probably wasn't the men who were at fault. She sometimes wondered if there was something within herself that was acting as a barrier to finding happiness and fulfilment. But she didn't have time to dwell on that right now. She had work to do, and that at least provided her with deep satisfaction.

She saw Matthew and Connor out a few minutes later. 'Perhaps I'll see you both at home later?' she said, waving them goodbye. Catherine's shopping trips usually went on for longer than an hour or so, which gave Matthew an excuse to come and visit.

Laura went in search of Tom, to find out whether he still needed help.

Nick was attending to Tom's burns patient, a young man, and Laura wondered where the consultant had gone.

'We'll get you transferred to the burns unit within the next hour,' Nick was saying. 'For the moment we'll keep the area moist and make sure that there's no danger of infection setting in. Just ask the nurse if you need more pain medication.'

He spoke quietly to the nurse, and then turned to Laura. Moving away from the cubicle, he said, 'I take it that your brother's gone home?'

'Yes. It didn't take long to fix him up.' She glanced around. 'Where's Tom?'

'He went to have a word with the patient's relatives. He'd done all that was necessary for his patient, but the family were anxious and needed reassurance.'

'He was coping all right, then? From what you said earlier, I thought there might be a problem looming.'

Nick shrugged. 'I guess I was wrong.'

Laura gave him a sideways glance. It wasn't like him to admit a mistake…or to make one, for that matter. 'It was thoughtful of you to send those jigsaws for Connor,' she murmured. 'They kept him amused for quite a while.'

His jaw moved in a faint grimace. 'Well, you know my feelings about this place and children. It isn't a good environment for them, and if I can brighten up the experience for them in any way, that's what I try to do. It's something I've mentioned to your father.'

'You could try approaching the Friends of the Hospital for funds. I'm sure if you put your case in a suitable fashion they would want to help in any way they could.'

'I think my plans would take more financing than they would be willing to provide. Besides, I believe that your father, being in administration, is the man who holds the key to unlock the funds. You'd think that since he was a consultant himself in A and E, he would know what needed to be done and he would have some sympathy for the changes I'm suggesting.'

Laura bridled at his tone. 'I'm sure that he does. After all, he was the one who set aside separate cubicles with resuscitation equipment especially for paediatric patients. When he was in charge there wasn't the money to do any more than that. Besides, he spearheaded the drive to get the public to donate funds for the MRI machine that the hospital has now. That took a lot of effort and persuasion and years of hard work. You don't give him enough credit for what he has done.'

Nick's eyes darkened. 'I accept that he did a good thing where the MRI machine was concerned. It's what he plans to do now that concerns me.'

'Whatever he does, it will be with the best of intentions,' she said sharply. 'If my father is cautious, you should realise that it's because he sees both sides of the coin.'

'You mean that he has to toe the management line. He's forgotten what it was like to be at the cutting edge of things.'

'That's unfair.'

'Is it?'

Laura's opened her mouth, ready to speak her mind, but just then Jenny hurried towards them.

'You have to come quickly, both of you,' she said breathlessly. 'It's Tom—I think he's having a bad angina attack. He's in the doctors' lounge. I've tried giving him his usual medication, but it's not working.'

'We're on our way.' Nick was already moving towards the door, and Laura was at his heels.

Tom Edwards was in his early sixties, a tall, thin man, with greying hair. Now he was slumped on the floor, beads of perspiration on his forehead and his face ashen.

'I left him in the chair while I went to get help,' Jenny said. 'The attack must have worsened while I was coming to find you. I've already given him aspirin.'

'Good thinking.' Nick was loosening Tom's tie and then he positioned him so that his upper body was elevated. Laura grabbed some cushions to help support him.

'Tom, can you hear me?' Nick spoke in a low, urgent voice and Tom made a faint movement of his head in acknowledgement.

'You'll be all right. We'll take care of you,' Nick said, beginning to make a swift examination. 'Are you in pain?'

Again, Tom managed to nod faintly. 'Chest. Bad.' He

began to choke, and Nick said quickly, 'Don't try to talk. We'll take care of you now.'

Tom subsided, and Nick turned swiftly to Laura. 'I'll intubate. Let's get him hooked up to oxygen quickly.' Glancing at Jenny, he said, 'We'll give him glycerine trinitrate sublingually to expand the arteries, and set up an infusion of isosorbide dinitrate. You had better do an ECG, and keep an eye on his blood pressure.'

'Will do.'

Laura was already starting an intravenous line. Tom looked to be in a bad way, and she was afraid that if they didn't work fast he would go into cardiac arrest. 'Are we giving beta-blockers and morphine?'

He nodded, working swiftly as he answered. 'I'll make arrangements for him to be admitted.'

Laura taped the IV line in place, and for the next few minutes they worked as a team to resuscitate their consultant.

'If he's not pain-free in forty-eight hours, they'll probably want to do coronary angiography. Given his condition over the last few months, I wouldn't be surprised if he ends up having bypass surgery. It's been a wonder to me that he's coped for this long.' His mouth tightened as he spoke, and Laura frowned.

'What do you mean?'

'I guessed this would happen one day,' Nick said under his breath. 'I've been telling him for a long time now that he should have opted for early retirement on health grounds, but he wouldn't listen.'

'Can you blame him for that? He's worked hard all his life to get where he is, and no one would lightly throw it all away.'

His mouth twisted. 'That's what your father said.

They're great friends, aren't they, he and Tom? He went out of his way to defend his actions.'

'Because he believed the medication was working.'

Nick shook his head. 'It's clear that it wasn't. I told Tom that he shouldn't be treating patients while he was ill, but he always said that we work as a team and that there would be enough warning of an impending attack for him to be able to hand over to someone else.'

Laura sent Tom a swift, anxious glance, but it was doubtful that their patient could hear what they were saying.

'That's true, though, isn't it?' she murmured. 'He put himself at risk by carrying on, but not his patients.'

'Like your father, you'll believe what you want to believe.'

Frowning, she looked up at Nick. Was he right? No matter what her reservations were about him, she had to respect him as a doctor. He was doing everything in his power to save Tom. He worked quickly and efficiently and he was very clear thinking. But, then, as he'd said, he'd seen this coming, hadn't he?

She said quietly, 'What about fibrinolytics?'

'That's probably a good idea,' he said in a low voice. 'We'll get the test results first, but there's no history of ulcer or recent surgery so they're probably advisable in this instance. We need to do whatever we can to unclog these arteries.'

As soon as they had Tom stabilised, Nick arranged for him to be transferred to the cardiac unit. Laura watched Tom being wheeled away a little later, and hoped fervently that he would be all right.

'At least we were on hand to treat him,' Nick said. 'If he had been on his own, I doubt whether he would have survived. As it is, he's in the best place.'

She had the feeling that he was trying to comfort her. 'I know. I haven't known him for very long but, even so, I get on very well with him. He's so kind and thoughtful, and he always has time for other people. He was very good to me when I started here.'

'He's good to everyone. His problem has always been that he works too hard, and doesn't pay enough attention to his own health. If he had done, he might have heeded some of the signs that things were going wrong. Perhaps now he will begin to listen.'

Laura bit her lip. She felt as though she was losing a friend and ally. In the few months that she had known him, Tom had always been steadfast in his concern for his colleagues and his patients, and now he was the one who needed support. What had happened to him this morning was serious and life-threatening, and now he must be feeling vulnerable and frightened.

'He's in good hands. Our cardiac unit is one of the best in the country.'

She nodded. 'I know. We deal with these kinds of incidents all the time, and that should make it easier for us to cope, but Tom is one of our own. He's not all that much older than my father. It sort of brings things home to you, and makes you think of how these things affect families.'

'That's true.' He was silent for a moment, then said in a musing tone, 'Talking of families, that was a nasty gash your brother had. Is he keen on DIY?'

'Not especially, but it makes a change from sitting behind a desk all day. He likes to dabble in all sorts of things that involve keeping busy, like gardening, decorating, sport.'

'What work does he do?'

'He works in a bank. He enjoys what he does, but he

says that having a desk job means he doesn't get enough exercise.'

'Then he wasn't interested in following family tradition and going into medicine?'

'No, not really.'

'He's very much like your father, physically. Has his lack of interest in medicine caused any friction? I know that David was particularly pleased when you decided to go to medical school.'

'Perhaps he was, but all he really wants is for us to be happy, whatever we decide to do.'

Nick looked at her curiously. 'I still think it's strange that you and your brother are so very different in appearance. I met your mother once, when she came to a function at the hospital, but you don't seem to take after her either.'

Laura gave a faint, wry smile. She had to give him full points for observation. 'You're perfectly right,' she said softly. 'The truth is, Matthew is their natural son, but I was adopted. It doesn't matter to me, because I don't really remember it being any other way. I love my father dearly, and I miss my mother more than words can say.'

She lowered her head slightly, remembering her adoptive mother. 'It was a great shock to all of us when she died.'

Nick frowned. 'I'm sorry. I didn't mean to upset you.'

She lifted her head and braced herself. 'That's all right, I'm fine. I've had more than a few years to get over the fact that she's gone. It's just that it was so unexpected. She was a good driver, but it was a foggy night and there were patches of ice on the road. That particular bend in the road was an accident black spot.

At least now they've made it safer by putting warning signs up.'

'She would have been proud to know that you passed your medical exams, and that you became a fully fledged doctor.'

'Yes, I believe she would…even though I may still have a lot to learn.' Remembering his comments on her junior status from a few days ago, she threw him a hooded glance, and perhaps her gibe hit home because his mouth twisted at the corners.

He didn't follow it up, though, because an emergency admission dragged them both back to work.

The thought still rankled in her mind, though. Whenever she was on duty at the same time as Nick, she felt that he was keeping an eye on her, and she often wondered if he was expecting her to fall flat on her face. A and E was a challenging speciality, and she was doing her level best to master it. You never knew what to expect, but she wanted to do her utmost for her patients, and she knew that she would go on learning for quite some time. She just didn't need Nick to remind her of that.

When she went back home that evening, Matthew was there with Connor. Her father was showing Connor how to colour pictures on the computer, and he looked up and smiled as she walked into the living room.

'Matthew tells me that you had to stitch his hand for him this morning. You'd think a doctor's son would be more careful, wouldn't you?'

Laura chuckled. 'You would, but this is Matthew we're talking about. He's always been slightly accident-prone. He gets absorbed in what he's doing, to the exclusion of everything else.' She sent Matthew a smiling glance. 'I take it that Catherine's not back from her shopping trip yet?'

He nodded. 'She phoned to say that she met up with a friend, and they're having a meal together to celebrate the friend's birthday. She'll be back later on this evening.'

'Would you like to stay for dinner with us?'

'That would be great. I'm sure Connor will enjoy spending some more time with both of you.'

Over dinner, she told her father what had happened to Tom.

'I heard about it,' her father said. 'It's a bad business. I like Tom. We've worked together for years, and he's always been a good friend to me.'

Matthew frowned. 'Is this the same Tom who goes fishing with you in the summer?'

'That's right. I'm sorry to see him brought down by something like this.' He sent Laura a quick glance. 'I'm glad that you and Nick were there to take care of him.'

'I think Nick was expecting it, to be honest. I knew that Tom had been unwell for some time, but I didn't know how bad it was.'

'Nick's more observant than most, I'll give him that. He's a very clear-headed young man, but he's very forthright in his views, too. He doesn't pull his punches, and he forgets that there is more than one side to most situations.' He frowned, his mouth tightening in a spasm of anger. 'We've had more than a few arguments over this very subject. He didn't think Tom should have still been working in A and E.'

'I know.'

'Sometimes it seems as though Nick is totally insensitive to what other people are going through. I can understand how Tom must have felt, faced with the thought of giving up his work. I know what it's like to have to give up a career in medicine. It isn't an easy thing to accept that your way of life, everything that you've worked for, has to come to an end. It can be a brutal blow, but Nick will never appreciate that.' There was a bitter edge to his words. 'For him it seems like a simple enough decision, but for Tom it was something he couldn't even bear to consider.'

'It's been forced on him now.'

'Yes. He'll have a lot of thinking to do over these next few months while he recovers his strength.'

He reached for the coffee-pot and filled his cup. 'Actually, I called in to see Tom before I came home this evening. He said that you'd been in to see him, too, and I think it's made him feel a lot more cheerful to know that he's surrounded by friends. He seemed resigned to the fact that he's not going to be able to avoid surgery.'

'A triple bypass would give him a new lease of life.'

'That's true enough.' He shook his head in grim reflection. 'It's a sad fact, but I can't see him being able to come back to work. He's only a year or so off retirement, and I think in the end he'll come around to the fact that he will have to accept his limitations.'

'That's probably true, but at least he'll have his family around him. That will be something for him to look forward to.'

Her father nodded. 'I'm sure he'll be glad of their support.' His expression was sombre. 'On the other hand, as far as we're concerned, this whole sorry business leaves us with something of a predicament.'

Laura looked at him curiously. 'What do you mean?'

'I mean that the A and E department has been left with no consultant in charge.'

'Yes, I had thought of that. I suppose, if Tom is ill

for any length of time, which seems likely, the hospital will have to appoint an acting consultant, a locum perhaps.'

'I don't imagine it will be easy to get someone suitable as a matter of urgency. What's most likely to happen is that Nick will be asked to stand in temporarily.' His features darkened. 'I expect he'll be glad enough to step into Tom's shoes. With nobody standing in his way, he'll have free rein, won't he? What is there to stop him from going after what he wants?'

Laura's eyes widened. 'You mean that he will be in charge?'

'Unfortunately, I think that's a strong possibility.'

Laura struggled to absorb that. Nick, in charge? While she respected him as a doctor, there was no way she would be happy for him to have overall control of her daily work situation. It was bad enough at the moment, when there seemed to be constant friction between them. She was forever having to bite her tongue when their sometimes heated disagreements threatened to get out of control. How would it be when he was the acting consultant?

And that was without even beginning to consider the damaging effect his sudden promotion would have on his working relationship with her father. The result would be calamitous and didn't bear thinking about.

CHAPTER THREE

LAURA wiped yet another name from the board. That was one more patient she had treated and discharged that night. How many more were there likely to be before her shift ended? It seemed as though she had already dealt with hundreds. Flexing her tired muscles, she reached for another treatment chart.

Wayne Golding was waiting in cubicle number four, and she went there now, drawing back the curtains.

'Hello, Mr Golding,' she greeted him. 'I'm Dr Brett.' She glanced at the chart, and added, 'I understand you've had a nasty gash to your hand. Perhaps I could have a look at it.'

'Oh, so you're finally ready for me, are you?' he snarled disagreeably. 'How long does it take for you doctors to get around to looking at your patients around here? I could have bled to death by now.'

Taken aback, Laura viewed him warily. He was a big man in his forties, with ruddy cheeks and nose in a well-worn face that made him look as though he had lived life to the full. He also reeked of alcohol.

'I'm sorry that you've been kept waiting. We've been very busy dealing with emergency patients elsewhere in the department.'

He glared at her, his body stiff and threatening, so that she surreptitiously looked towards the alarm button. 'I haven't seen any emergency activity around here. I think you're just making excuses. I've got better things to do than sit around for hours on end.'

'I'm sure you have,' Laura said, hanging onto her patience by a thin thread. 'No one enjoys having to wait, but I can assure you that if we had made our road accident patients wait, they certainly wouldn't have lived to see the day out.' Her chin lifted in a determined and businesslike way. 'Perhaps if you let me take a look at your hand I'll be able to see what needs to be done and send you on your way.'

He thrust his hand towards her face so that she took a step backwards. 'It's obvious what needs to be done, isn't it?' He spoke to her as though he thought she was an idiot. 'It needs stitching up.'

She inspected the wound. His knuckles were lacerated, the skin split in several places. She probed gently, searching for any injury to the underlying tendons and ligaments. Growling, he pulled his hand away.

'Watch what you're doing. You don't need to maul it like that,' he snarled. 'For all you know, it could be broken.'

'I'm sorry if I hurt you,' Laura said quietly. 'Have you been in a fight?'

'Someone came at me and I let him have it. If my hand's broken, he's going to pay for this.'

'Fortunately the X-rays don't show any broken bones,' Laura murmured. 'The downside is that there is a nasty infection in there, possibly from an old wound.'

His eyes narrowed on her suspiciously. 'So what does that mean?'

'It means that I'll need to wash the wound out with a medicated solution, and then I'll put a dressing on your hand so that it stays clean. I'll prescribe an antibiotic as well to clear up the infection.'

'You mean you're not going to stitch it up?' Angrily, he got to his feet, and Laura quickly drew back, startled.

'I'm afraid I can't, not while there's an infection present. You'll need to come back the day after tomorrow so that we can look at it again.'

'You're doing this to wind me up.' He lunged towards her, his face a mask of aggression.

'I'm not, I promise you.' She tried to stay calm, but his anger was making her feel uncomfortable. 'If you'll excuse me for just a moment, I'll go and get some supplies.'

Without giving him any chance to object, she walked out of the cubicle and drew the curtains behind her. Pulling in a sharp breath, she went to the desk at the far end of the room and began to count soundlessly to ten.

'Is there a problem?' Nick flicked a glance over her, appraising her carefully from head to toe.

'None at all.' The last thing she needed was to admit to Nick that she was having difficulty treating a patient. He placed a lot of emphasis on treating patients with respect. Pain sometimes made people unreasonable, he had said, and it was their job in A and E to look beyond a person's critical or tetchy comments.

'Really?' he said drily. 'I heard someone shouting. Are you having trouble with a patient?'

'It's nothing that I can't handle,' she said tersely.

'I'd still prefer it if you'd told me what's going on,' he persisted. 'It's late at night, and we're busy in the department. Tempers get frayed, and things can easily get out of hand.'

Laura grimaced. He thought she was going to mess

things up, didn't he? That wouldn't go down well. Tom Edwards had been easygoing and tolerant, but Nick was a different animal altogether. Over these last few weeks, while he'd been in charge of A and E, he had made it clear that he liked things to run smoothly, and he was keen on keeping the department up to full speed.

'I won't let that happen.'

'You came on duty tonight to help out because we were short-handed, didn't you? This isn't your usual shift.'

'That's right.' She looked at him steadily. 'What difference does that make?'

'It means that you haven't had much of a break between shifts, and I know that you haven't had a coffee-break for some time. I think you should go and get one now.'

'I'm in the middle of treating a patient, or had you forgotten?'

'I'll deal with him.'

Laura shook her head. 'I would prefer to do that myself. It's a matter of professional pride.'

His mouth crooked in a half-smile. 'You can be a very stubborn woman at times, can't you?'

'I prefer to use the word independent.' She moved away from him towards a cupboard. 'If you'll excuse me, I need to get some supplies.'

He watched her go, and Laura turned her attention to getting the irrigation equipment. It took her a few minutes to find what she needed, and when she returned to the cubicle where she had left Wayne Golding, she was startled to see that Nick was already in there.

'I hope you understand what I've been saying,' Nick murmured, giving Wayne a narrow-eyed look. 'That's a nasty infection, but Dr Brett will clean it up for you and make arrangements for a follow-up appointment. Now I have other patients to attend to. Goodbye, Mr Golding.'

Wayne looked uncomfortable, and Laura wondered what on earth had been going on. She sent Nick a questioning glance, but he simply swept determinedly past her and went to check on another patient.

Wayne was subdued as she washed out the wound on his hand, and he made no murmur when she carefully taped a dressing in place. The change in his attitude was remarkable, and Laura had no idea what had brought about the transformation. He even thanked her when she passed him on to a nurse who would arrange his follow-up appointment.

The whole episode puzzled her so much that she went in search of Nick. He was treating a pneumothorax, and she assisted him until they were both sure that their patient was out of danger.

'Would you like to tell me what you said to Wayne Golding?' she asked as they cleaned up afterwards. 'He was a different man when I went back to treat him.'

'I heard what he had been saying to you, so I simply told him that his behaviour wouldn't be tolerated. The doctors and nurses in A and E have a difficult enough job to do, and they deserve respect. I made it clear to him that if he couldn't control his temper and behave in a reasonable fashion, I would ask Security to remove him from the premises.'

Her jaw dropped. 'You really said that? But I thought you would blame me for not handling the situation efficiently and sending him on his way.'

He frowned. 'Why on earth would you think that?'

'Things have been so different around here since Tom

was taken ill, and I'm not always sure that I'm doing the right thing. The triage system is different, and the working rotas have changed. We assess patients, treat them and mostly we send them on their away more quickly than before, but it isn't always possible.'

'Don't you think it's a good thing that we've made the department more efficient?'

'Yes, I do, but the changes have happened so quickly, and I'm not sure whether you expect one hundred per cent efficiency. I'm not certain that that's attainable.'

'Then perhaps we should get one thing straight at the outset. I value the co-operation of all the staff in A and E. Everyone has worked tremendously hard to make the department function efficiently, but it could be that I've been concentrating so hard on getting things off the ground that I haven't made it clear to everyone how much I appreciate what they have done. I need to remedy that.'

Nick frowned. 'I still don't understand why you didn't come to me with any of your doubts.'

She made a wry smile. 'I'm just a junior doctor here, remember. I value my job and I don't want to rock the boat unnecessarily.'

'Laura,' he said in a dry tone, 'I'm here to support you in what you do. If you have any problems, you should bring them to me. You're not expected to manage things on your own. We work as a team. That's one of the fundamental characteristics of working in A and E.'

'Maybe, but you always seem to expect perfection. It's sometimes hard to live up to the standards that you set.'

He turned his gaze on her. 'Are you sure that I'm the one who expects perfection?' He shook his head, his glance trailing over the oval of her face in such an intent fashion that she felt her cheeks flush with heat. 'I think you underestimate yourself, Laura. You're the one who sets yourself an impossible standard. You're so worried that you will do something wrong that you can't let yourself relax. You're a good doctor, and you should have confidence in yourself, but we're only human, and even the best of us will sometimes make mistakes, especially if we're overtired and overworked.'

He laid a hand lightly on her shoulder and turned her towards the doctors' lounge. 'That's why I suggested that you should go and get yourself some coffee. Not because I thought you had done anything wrong, but because you needed to give yourself time to calm down and get things into perspective. Don't you think that's reasonable?'

Laura didn't know what she thought just then. She wasn't used to having him quite so close, and it was becoming increasingly difficult for her to concentrate when his arm was draped around her like that. It was a totally innocuous gesture, but the warmth of his hand permeated the thin cotton top that she was wearing, and his gentle touch was doing unbelievably strange things to her insides. She was suddenly overwhelmingly aware of him as a man, in a way that she never had been before. He was powerfully masculine and his nearness made her feel utterly feminine and vulnerable all at once.

'Laura?'

'Yes…yes, of course, you're right.' She swallowed. 'It can be difficult to get a true perspective of things when you're overtired.' She had worked two shifts close together and she had been on duty for too long, that was why she was feeling this way. It had nothing to do with the fact that he was holding her. She was just being fanciful because she was tired and overwrought.

'We've been working at a punishing pace, and you haven't had a break since you came on duty. That isn't good for anyone, and you owe it to yourself to take some time out.'

'I will,' she said. 'Anyway, there's only another hour to go until my shift ends. Perhaps things will quieten down a bit and we can all relax.'

'It's always bad when the pubs close, but things are easing up already. We've worked our way through most of the cases. Now it's time for you to go and take a breather. I don't want to see you back in the department for at least another twenty minutes.'

'Yes, sir.' She gave him a mock salute and his blue-grey eyes flashed a warning.

'Don't push your luck,' he said drily.

She didn't see very much of Nick over the next few days since lately their shifts rarely coincided, and it was the same on the following weekend. Laura was on duty in A and E when they had news of a road traffic accident.

'The paramedics are bringing a woman in,' Sarah, the nurse who was working with her, said. 'She's eight months pregnant and she was involved in a collision with another car. She's begun to have contractions.'

'Why aren't they taking her straight to Maternity?'

'She has an injury. Query a fracture of the wrist.'

'OK. Let's get the ultrasound equipment in here, and we'd better get everything ready for an emergency birth, just in case the baby should decide to arrive early. I'll examine her and then we'll send her straight to X-Ray so that we can see what we're dealing with. I think we should notify the obstetric team in case we need to get someone down here urgently.'

Alison Jenkins was brought in just a few moments later. She was a young woman, in her early twenties, and she was obviously distressed and in pain. Laura went straight to her and tried to reassure her.

'You're in safe hands now, Alison. We'll try to make you as comfortable as we can.' Beginning a careful examination, Laura said quietly, 'Can you tell me what happened?'

'I was on my way to collect my daughter from her childminder. I work weekends in a store, part time, and I'd finished for the day. Someone pulled out from a side road and smashed straight into me. I saw it coming and I tried to avoid it, but he was going too fast.' She bit down on her lip as another contraction came. 'The baby's coming too soon, isn't it? It isn't due for another month.' Panic made her voice shake.

'Don't worry about that. You're in the best place if anything does start to happen. We'll take care of you.' Laura listened to the foetal heartbeat. 'That sounds fine,' she murmured. She judged that labour was too far advanced for her to be able to stop it from happening. 'I'll give you something to relieve the pain,' she added. 'The contractions are still some distance apart, so we have time to look at your wrist and find out what's happened there.'

'Will you get somebody to ring the childminder for me? I need to know that Katie will be looked after. She's only two years old, and I don't want her fretting. I need to know that she's all right.'

Laura nodded. 'Of course. We'll sort that out right away.' She signalled to a nurse to take care of that side of things, and then turned her attention to Alison's wrist. 'Is there anyone else you want us to ring—your husband, perhaps?'

Alison shook her head. 'No... I don't want him around. We separated when he discovered that I was pregnant again.' She pulled a face. 'He can't handle being a father.'

Laura grimaced. 'I'm sorry. What about the rest of your family—is there someone else we can contact for you?'

'I don't have any family. There's just Katie and me. I need to know that she's all right.'

Laura sensed that Alison was getting agitated again. 'Try to calm yourself.' It wouldn't do Alison or the baby any good if her blood pressure shot through the roof. 'We'll deal with all that for you.'

From her examination, she discovered that there was pain and swelling over the radial aspect of the wrist, and that Alison had problems with her grip.

Laura said gently, 'Thankfully, you have no other injuries apart from your wrist, so we can concentrate on that for the time being. But I think I should wait until after the baby is born before giving you an X-ray.'

Quietly, she took Sarah to one side and said, 'Could you do me a favour and strap her wrist up to make her as comfortable as possible? I have to make a call but then I'll be back to do an ultrasound.'

Sarah nodded. 'That's fine, leave it to me.'

Laura made an urgent call to the obstetric department. 'I need someone to come down to A and E to look at a patient who is in labour,' she said.

'I'm sorry, but there's no one available just yet,' a doctor told her. 'The consultant is off duty this weekend, and doesn't appear to have her mobile phone switched on, so we can't contact her. The rest of the team are involved with emergencies here. You'll have to cope as best you can for the time being.'

Laura put the receiver down and wondered what she ought to do next. The senior A and E doctor was working on a critically injured patient, and she couldn't pull him away from that.

Sarah finished the strapping within minutes, and Laura hurried to examine Alison once more. By this time the contractions were much closer together.

'How are you feeling, Alison? I hope the strapping has made your wrist a little more comfortable for you.'

'It feels easier, thanks. Is there any news about Katie?'

'Your childminder says she'll keep her for as long as necessary. She said not to worry, Katie's fine.'

Relieved, Alison sank back against her pillows while Laura examined her. She was becoming increasingly concerned about Alison's condition. This time she found tenderness in her abdomen. Laura also noted that Alison's features were pale and that she looked as though she was about to faint. Laura began to be afraid that she might be bleeding internally.

'Alison, I'm going to give you oxygen,' she said gently. 'It will help you to breathe more easily, and it will make sure that the baby gets a better supply.'

The foetus was beginning to show signs of distress, and Laura decided that it was time to find out exactly what was causing the problems.

'The ultrasound scan,' she told Alison, 'is going to let me see what's happening with the baby. Bear with me, I know that you're feeling uncomfortable.'

The result was what she had feared. The scan showed

that the placenta had become detached from the wall of the uterus and Alison was beginning to haemorrhage. Once the placenta became completely detached, the foetus would no longer be supplied with sufficient oxygen.

Turning to Sarah, Laura said in a low voice, 'Put out another call for someone from the obstetric team to come down here urgently, will you?'

Sarah hurried away and Laura set about reassuring her patient. 'What I'm going to do now, Alison, is to give you some fluids intravenously. That should help you to feel a lot better.'

By the time the line was in place, Sarah had returned. She shook her head slightly and said quietly, 'No luck, I'm afraid. There's still no one available.'

Laura absorbed the information worriedly. 'OK. Stay with Alison and monitor her condition. If there is any change call me immediately. I'm going to see if I can contact Nick.'

Nick answered the phone within moments, and Laura felt a huge flood of relief wash through her at the sound of his voice. 'What's the problem?' he asked.

Quickly, Laura explained. 'It isn't a situation that I've had to deal with before. What should I be doing?'

'From the sound of it, you're doing everything that's possible at the moment. You need to make sure that she doesn't go into shock. That would be very dangerous for both her and the baby. Keep her warm. If her condition deteriorates, she'll need to deliver the baby quickly, by Caesarean, so you should have a theatre standing by. In the meantime, try tilting the bed at the foot. That can sometimes help.'

'But I've never done a Caesarean,' Laura said, trying to keep the alarm from her voice.

'I'm on my way in,' Nick said. 'Just try to keep calm, and go on reassuring your patient.'

He was on his way. Laura pulled in a deep breath. That simple statement made her feel so much better. Nick would know what to do.

She went back to her patient and checked the fluids that were being administered, and gave Alison an epidural so that the anaesthesia would be in place if surgery became inevitable. Then she tilted the bed as Nick had suggested.

He arrived just a few minutes later, hurrying into the department and shrugging into his theatre scrubs at top speed. Alison was in a bad way.

'She isn't fully dilated,' Laura told him. 'There's no way that she can deliver this baby normally, but I'm anxious about her condition and that of the baby.'

'We'll get her to Theatre as soon as possible,' he said. 'Is everything organised?'

'Yes, I've seen to it.' She paused, and then added, 'I'm sorry that I had to call you out on your weekend off, but I'm so thankful that you came in to help out. I don't know how I would have managed without you.'

'We're all in a difficult situation now that Tom is out of action. The department's been left in a state of limbo while we wait to know what's going to happen. The bypass operation was successful by all accounts, but we still don't know whether or not he will be coming back to work. It hasn't been easy to find a locum consultant to ease the situation either. In the meantime, I'll do what I can to support everyone.'

'Thank you. I'm really grateful to you.'

Nick went over to the bed and introduced himself to Alison. 'Hello, Alison. I'm Nick Hilliard.'

He examined her briefly. 'It looks as though this baby is rather anxious to be born,' he commented, 'and I think we need to give it a helping hand. What I propose to do is to take you along to Theatre and deliver your baby by Caesarean section. That way we can take care of both you and the baby in the best way possible. Are you happy about that—do you have any questions that you want to ask me?'

Alison shook her head. 'I just want what's for the best for my baby. Please, don't let anything happen to it.'

'We'll look after you and your baby, I promise.' He turned to Laura. 'Let's get this mother and baby up to Theatre right away.'

Laura was amazed at how quickly things progressed after that. As soon as they arrived in Theatre, Nick worked with supreme skill, as though this was the sort of thing he did every day. A screen was set up across the mother's waist, and then Nick made a five-inch incision low down on her abdomen and sucked out the amniotic fluid. He lifted out the baby while gently pressing down on Alison's stomach.

The baby appeared lifeless for a moment or two, and Laura held her breath and watched anxiously while the theatre nurse quickly cleaned up the infant. She found herself sending up a silent prayer. Please, let her be all right… She has to be… Then, after what seemed like an age, the baby's skin began to pink up and she uttered a small cry of protest.

Laura jerked into action but a few moments later, she realised that Alison's condition was deteriorating. 'Nick, her blood pressure's falling…'

'She is haemorrhaging badly,' Nick said under his

breath. 'I need to get this bleeding under control. Let's get more fluids into her now.'

Nick worked fast but, despite his efforts, Alison suddenly collapsed and went into cardiac arrest. Laura was stunned. She couldn't lose her patient. It was unbearable to think that she had just brought a child into the world and now it was all coming to an end. It couldn't be happening…she wouldn't let it happen.

The whole team suddenly launched into action. Laura swiftly put an endotracheal tube and airway in place and connected them to an oxygen supply, while Nick charged the defibrillator.

'I'm going to shock the heart,' Nick said. 'Stand clear…'

The team stood back, and Laura's stomach knotted painfully while she waited for the cardiac monitor to show signs that he had been successful. Was Alison going to pull through? She must. Her baby was crying for her, and the sound tugged at Laura's heart with an intensity that she hadn't known before. She thought of little Katie, waiting fretfully for her mother to return, and suddenly she couldn't cope with the prospect of these infants being left motherless. The thought paralysed her, made her unable to think, unable to act.

'Laura—are you with us?' Nick's sharp tone jerked her back to reality and the immediacy of the theatre.

'Yes…yes, of course.'

'I'm glad to hear it,' he said on a terse note. 'Keep an eye on the site of the haemorrhage.'

'We've got a pulse,' the nurse said, and the monitor began to record a heart rhythm. Laura began to breathe again.

'The bleeding's coming under control at last,' she commented.

Nick nodded. 'Let's keep up those fluids.' He checked that all was well before he began the careful task of suturing the wall of Alison's womb and then her abdomen.

He kept an eye on Alison's vital signs, and when he was satisfied he said, 'I think we're out of the woods for the time being. She can go through to the recovery room now. Thanks, everyone, you all did a great job.'

While Alison was in the recovery room, Laura decided to go and check on the baby. The past hour or so had been horrendous, and she was still shaken by her experience in the theatre, but at least she had the satisfaction of knowing that Alison and her baby had pulled through.

The baby was doing all right, and Laura sat with her, holding her tenderly in her arms. Tears burned behind her eyelids. 'Poor baby,' she whispered. 'I thought we were going to lose you and your mother. That was much too close for comfort.'

As she cradled the infant, the door opened and Nick walked in.

'I thought I might find you in here,' he said. 'Are you all right? You looked as though you were in shock back there in Theatre. I was worried for a while that you weren't going to be able to cope.'

'I'm fine,' she mumbled, hoping that he couldn't hear the tremor in her voice. 'I thought that we were going to lose Alison, and it was hard for me to deal with that. I couldn't bear the thought of this baby being motherless.'

She was still feeling upset and she didn't know how

to account for that. It wasn't a very professional attitude, and it was no wonder that Nick was concerned. What must he be thinking?

He was studying her expression thoughtfully. 'It was worrying for a time, I agree. No one wants to lose a patient, especially a young mother like that. But your fears for the baby were probably unfounded. She would have been all right in the end, wouldn't she? There are always people queuing up to adopt.'

His tone was brisk and matter-of-fact, but Laura couldn't accept his argument. What did he know about motherless children?

'I don't think it's quite as simple as you're suggesting.'

'Isn't it? You've been through the experience of losing your natural mother, and as far as I can tell you seem to have come out of it relatively unscathed. Or is that not true? Is that why you reacted so badly when Alison was in danger? Were you thinking about what happened to you when you were small?'

He was still watching her and the realisation that he had hit a nerve was making her feel uncomfortable. Giving herself time to think, she gently stroked the baby's cheek, but her fingers were trembling so badly that she stopped, contenting herself with wrapping the blanket more securely around the infant instead.

Laura said slowly, 'I suppose the shock of what happened took me back to my own childhood for a few moments. I wasn't expecting to feel like that, and for a while I couldn't think clearly at all. Yes, you would imagine that adoption is the answer, but nothing about the process is as cut and dried as you imagine. It doesn't always mean that problems melt away.'

'I can't see that there would be that many problems where a small baby is concerned. An older child perhaps, but most people who are looking to adopt seem to want babies.'

'You make it sound so straightforward and trouble-free, but I don't think it works like that,' she said with a frown. 'There are all sorts of problems that can arise afterwards. Some children may not even discover they were adopted until they grow up, and then the news comes as a shock to them. There are those who start to wonder about the circumstances of their adoption, and want to find out more about their natural parents. That doesn't always work out too well.'

'Is that how you feel?'

'Sometimes,' she admitted. 'I wasn't told that I was adopted until I was about ten years old. I think my mother was afraid that it might change things if I knew the truth, but she was wrong in that. I love my adoptive parents dearly and I wouldn't have changed them for the world. But there are times when I wonder about my natural parents, and want to know more about them.'

'Have you tried to find them?'

'Not really. Not yet. I have thought about it, but when my mother—my adoptive mother—was alive I didn't want to upset her, to appear disloyal, and after she died I was too busy with my medical training to do anything about it.'

'Couldn't your father tell you anything about them?'

'He has talked to me about it in the past, but I always feel as though something is missing. There is always something else that I want to know.'

'Perhaps you should talk to him some more, try to clear up any questions that are troubling you. What happened today in Theatre could happen again, you know, and the next time you're distracted there might be serious consequences for your patient. It's possible that your father may have the answers you're looking for.'

She shook her head. 'I'm not sure that it would be a good idea to talk to him about it. I've always sensed that he doesn't want to dwell on the subject.'

'Why should it be a problem for him? You're the one who's being affected by the situation.'

'I'm not certain. Perhaps, deep down, he might be hurt because I still feel the need to know about my real parents, even after all that he has done for me over the years. I know he used to worry that any discussion might upset my mother. I just don't want to upset him.'

'Isn't it about time you thought about what's right for you? Your father is a grown man. He should be able to handle any problems that come his way.'

She grimaced. 'I might have known you'd take that attitude. It wouldn't bother you if my father was upset, would it? You don't like him very much, do you?'

Nick shrugged. 'I didn't say that. This has nothing to do with my relationship with your father. I'm just saying that if you have a problem that's affecting your work, you should face up to it and do something about it, instead of letting it niggle away in the background.'

A nurse came into the room. 'Apparently Alison is recovering some of her strength now, and she's asking about her baby. I thought I'd better get you to come and check her over first, Laura.'

'Good. I'm glad she's feeling well enough to ask. Do you want to take care of the baby while I go and see her?'

The nurse nodded and came forward and Laura carefully handed her the precious bundle. Getting to her feet, she said, 'I'll go and have a word with her, and find out if she's up to it.'

She looked around for Nick, to see if he wanted to go with her, but he was already striding out of the room.

Alison was propped up in bed in the recovery room. She looked much better, considering what she had been through.

'How are you feeling?' Laura asked, making a swift examination of her. 'You had us all worried for a while.'

'Much better, thanks, but the nurse says that I'll have to stay in hospital for a while.'

'Yes, we'll have to admit you so that we can keep an eye on you. We've also got to get that wrist X-rayed and bandaged up properly. We can make arrangements for Katie to be brought in to see you, if you like.'

Alison looked relieved. 'What about my baby?' she asked.

'You have a beautiful little girl,' Laura murmured, giving Alison a smile. 'Would you like to hold her?'

Alison nodded, and Laura signalled to the nurse to bring the baby into the room. Alison held out her arms for the infant.

Laura watched as she gently stroked the baby's cheek and drew her down against her chest.

'Have you decided on a name for her?' Laura asked.

Alison nodded. 'I'm going to call her Vicky, after my mother.'

'That's a lovely name.'

The theatre nurse came in just then, and said, 'Alison, you have a friend waiting for you outside. Someone called Jason? He wants to know if you are feeling up to having visitors?'

Alison's eyes widened. 'Jason is here?' She looked thoughtful for a moment, and then explained, 'He lives close by to me. He's been really nice to me these last few months. I expect my childminder told him what was happening. I had no idea that he would want to come and see me here.'

'Shall we get you tidied up and onto a ward?' Laura queried. 'If you feel up to it, Jason could stay with you for a few minutes.'

'I think I would like that,' Alison said softly.

Laura's shift came to an end a short time later, and she decided to go and look in on Tom. He was still in the cardiac care unit, and when she had last seen him he had been making a slow but steady recovery.

'Tom,' she greeted him. 'How are you?' He was hooked up to a monitor, and there were tubes attached to him, since his operation was still fairly recent.

He smiled at her. 'I'm feeling all right, thanks, but I'll be much better in a day or so when these tubes are removed.'

'I expect you will.' She sat down beside his bed. 'I brought some books for you to read, and some fruit.'

'Bless you.' He looked at the selection of paperbacks. 'I can see that you've been talking to Sandra,' he said with a smile.

Laura nodded. 'Your wife told me the kind of thing you enjoy reading. She said she didn't think you had read any of these titles yet.'

They talked for a while longer, until Laura sensed that he needed to rest. 'It's time I went home,' she told him. 'I'm glad to see that you're on the mend. We all miss you so much. We want you back on your feet again.'

'Ah, well, that's what I want, too. Sandra has things all worked out, you know. She tells me that I'm to take early retirement on health grounds, and she's planning a holiday for us. She reckons I've worked hard enough over the years and now it's time to stop.'

'How do you feel about that?'

He hesitated. 'On the whole, I think she's probably right. I've had plenty of time to think things through over these last few weeks, and I know now that I should have done it long ago. I was too stubborn to see it. I convinced myself that I was indestructible and thought I could go on and on.'

He gave a dry smile. 'Well, I was wrong, and now retirement has been forced on me, one way and another. I know that I'm never going to be a hundred per cent fit again, but the bypass will have given me a new lease of life. Sandra and I will be able to enjoy our retirement together.'

'We shall all miss you.'

'And I shall miss all of you, and this place, but it will give some of the young bloods a chance to run the department. Like Nick, for instance. That's if he hasn't already accepted the post he applied for in Somerset. I know they're really keen for him to make a start down there.'

Laura was startled. 'I didn't know that he was looking for another job. It was rumoured, of course, but I didn't know that he had actually done anything about it.'

'Between you and me, Laura, I gave him a reference and he went for an interview last week. I wish him all the luck in the world, although I think this hospital management would be foolish to let him go. He deserves to get on. He's passed all the relevant exams with excellent results, and a post as a consultant would be the next rung up the ladder for him. I can't see that there's anything to hold him back.'

Laura went out to the car park a few minutes later, deep in thought. Her father had hinted that something like this might be in the offing, but she hadn't really believed that it would come about.

'Did I just see you coming from the cardiac care unit?' Nick drew level with her as she walked to her car.

'That's right. I went to see how Tom is doing.' She sent him a quick glance, trying to fathom what might be going on in that intelligent, energetic mind of his.

'He's told you, hasn't he? About the job?' He gave a rueful smile. 'I can see it in your eyes.'

'I'd already heard something on the grapevine, but these things aren't always accurate.'

'This one is. They offered me the post when I went for the interview.'

Laura stared at him. 'Did you accept?'

Nick smiled wryly. 'I told them that I would think about it,' he said. 'Would you miss me if I went away?' he asked teasingly. 'You and I don't always see things in the same light, do we? I expect you would heave a big sigh of relief.'

'That's a strong possibility,' she told him.

In truth, though, she didn't know how she would feel if he left. Whenever she thought about him a mixture of strange sensations rampaged through her, and she didn't understand why she reacted this way. Now that he was close by, she felt hot and cold at the same time, and her pulse was shooting into overdrive. What could account for the strange lurch in her chest?

They had reached her car by now, and she stopped to unlock the door.

He watched her. 'Management has asked me if I would consider a post as consultant here if Tom decides not to stay on.'

Startled, she looked up at him. 'And what did you say to that?'

'I told them it was a bit premature for them to be offering Tom's job while he was still recovering from his surgery, and that if I did consider taking it on at some future date, there would have to be a whole lot of changes around here. I outlined some of them.'

'So you've given them something to think about?'

'I'd say so, yes.' He smiled and gave her a slight nod. 'I'll see you tomorrow.'

Laura watched him walk to his sleek silver saloon just a short distance away. She felt as though she was caught between the devil and the deep blue sea. Why was she feeling in such a confused state of mind? Was she hoping that he would stay?

CHAPTER FOUR

NICK was in vigorous form. He had a smile and a cheery word for each of his patients as he moved about the department, and that was nothing unusual, but today his sheer energy made Laura wince. If only she had half his stamina.

He must have noticed her looking in his direction, because he queried lightly, 'You're looking a bit under the weather. Did you have a bad night?'

She blinked. How did he know that? She thought she had been making a fairly good job of disguising her weariness.

'So-so.' She stiffened her shoulders and sent him a cool look. 'It doesn't mean that I'm not capable of doing my work efficiently.'

'I wasn't criticising,' he said drily. 'There's no need for you to be defensive...unless, of course, your conscience is troubling you.'

Laura made a face. That was just it, wasn't it? She always seemed to be on the defensive around Nick.

'It isn't.' He was still studying her, and she gave up trying to hide the truth. 'In fact, if you must know, my brother and his wife came over last night, with Connor. We had a good time, but Connor fell asleep and they all decided to stay over. They had both had a drink and didn't want to drive back.'

'That sounds like a sensible decision.'

'I thought so.'

'So were you up half the night, talking?'

Laura shook her head. 'I would hardly do that, not when I had to come to work the next day. What actually happened was that Connor had the room next to mine, but for some reason he was a bit restless in the early hours and I had to get up a couple of times to soothe him. It was just one of those things. If I could have had just a couple more hours' sleep I would have been all right.'

'What was wrong with him?'

Laura frowned, remembering the way she had stroked the little boy's fair hair as he lay in bed, trying to soothe him. 'He seemed to be a little feverish, and he was complaining of a headache.'

'Could it be a virus?'

'Possibly. I suggested to Catherine that she give him some infant paracetamol to ease the pain and bring his temperature down. I expect she'll take him to see her GP if he doesn't get any better—though the surgery's only open for a couple of hours today, with it being the weekend.'

'Children are down one minute and up the next. I don't suppose it's anything to worry about.'

He glanced at his watch, and Laura said, 'Are you off somewhere?'

He nodded. 'I have a meeting with management in fifteen minutes. Richard will be in charge while I'm away, so if you have any problems you'll need to refer them to him.'

'I'll do that.' She wasn't too happy about working with Richard Caldwell, though she didn't tell Nick that. Richard was a locum doctor, well qualified, and confident in himself, but Laura thought he was sometimes too quick in his assessments of patients.

She wondered if Nick's meeting was another interview for the consultant post, but Nick was on the move again before she had time to ask him.

Instead, she sounded her father out when he came into the department a while later.

'I imagine that's what it's about. I know that they aren't likely to find someone of the right calibre all that easily. If Nick decides to accept the job in Somerset then quite frankly it will leave us in chaos. Unfortunately, there's no one around who's as capable as he is.' He grimaced. 'Management is well aware of what a marvellous job he's done to keep down waiting times and keep the department running smoothly while Tom has been ill.'

'But if he's appointed to the job here, he would really shake the place up, wouldn't he? Where would that leave you?'

He winced. 'It will be a headache, there's no denying it. There would be no stopping him once he has the consultant post. He and I don't see eye to eye on things as it is, but I suppose we'll just have to try to talk our differences through. I can't see any other way round it.'

'At least you look stronger these days. I've been worried about you lately. That virus took it out of you, but perhaps you're turning the corner now. It's beginning to look as though you've made a full recovery.'

'I'm fine, Laura.' He gave her a smile. 'You worry too much, you know. Though I must say it's been like a tonic, having you back home these last few months.'

Laura returned the smile. 'For me, too.'

He started back towards his office a few minutes later, and Laura saw that he stopped on the way to pass the time of day with Jenny and the other nurses. He had always got on well with the staff, and she knew that he was always there for them, ready to help out with their problems or to share their joys. He was a good man.

She went to find her next patient, and was kept busy for the next hour or so dealing with a man who had suffered a chemical burn to his arm.

She was surprised when she came back from her lunch-break to see her sister-in-law, Catherine, in the waiting room with Connor.

'Hello, Catherine,' she said, going over to them. 'Is everything all right?'

'Not really. Connor still doesn't look well, and I'm worried about him. I couldn't get to see my own doctor because the surgery's closed today. All I could think to do was to bring him here, but one of the doctors has already looked at him. That was some time ago. About an hour or more. He said he didn't think it was anything more than a simple viral infection, so I started for home. Then I had second thoughts because Connor really doesn't look well, and I don't know what to do. I think it's more than that, so I came back here and waited to see if I could have a word with you.'

Laura glanced at Connor. He looked feverish, not at all himself, and she could see why Catherine was worried.

Lethargically, he waved a paper in front of her. 'I bringed you a picture,' he said.

Laura smiled at him and then turned her attention to the picture, which looked like a box on top of a box with wobbly circles underneath. 'It's lovely,' she told him, wondering what it was supposed to be.

'It's a tractor,' he said tiredly.

She nodded. 'I can see it is.' There was a squiggle in one of the boxes, a circle and a couple of sticks. 'And there's the driver at the front,' she said with a smile. 'You are clever.'

She knelt down beside him so that she was on a level with him. 'Do you still have your headache, Connor?' she asked.

He nodded slowly, as though it hurt him to do that. He was squinting a little, too, Laura noticed, and wondered whether that was because of the pain.

'Do you know which doctor you saw?' she asked Catherine.

'I think it was Dr Caldwell.'

'I'll have a look at Dr Caldwell's notes,' Laura said. 'Bring Connor through to the treatment room. I can examine him better in there.'

Catherine stood up. She reached down to lift Connor and carry him in her arms, and Laura could see that Connor was in no state to walk by himself. Looking at him, she was surprised he'd even had the strength to draw a picture, but then she recalled that he'd been doing it the previous evening.

Laura showed them into a cubicle that had been set aside for paediatric cases. She gently examined Connor, and while she was doing that he suddenly started to retch. Laura found a basin just in time.

'It's all right, Connor. Don't worry.' She gently wiped his face. 'Were you sick before you came here this morning?'

The child didn't answer, but flopped against his mother. Then he mumbled something, and Laura realised that he was a little confused.

She was worried about him. 'I'm going to give him some penicillin, just be on the safe side,' Laura told Catherine. 'I'll just go and get the things that I need. I won't be a moment.'

She drew back the curtains and went to get a syringe and medication.

Richard frowned at her as she left the cubicle. 'What's that little boy doing in there? I discharged him just a short time ago.'

'He's my nephew,' Laura explained. 'His mother's worried about him.'

'I dare say she is, but I've already told her that he has a simple viral infection.'

'I know, but he looks very poorly now. I'm concerned that but there might be something more serious wrong with him, like some form of meningitis. I just want to take precautions so that we can avert any problems.'

'Nonsense. I appreciate that he's your nephew, and that you want to do the right thing by him, but we're not running a family welfare centre here. You should send him home. We have other patients to attend to.'

'I can't move him now because he's just been sick, and he may be again. I want to make sure that he's a little more comfortable.'

'He'll feel better when he's at home, tucked up in bed. He shouldn't be here. Clean him up and send him on his way. Is that clear?'

'Yes, it's very clear.'

Laura anguished over the dilemma she found herself in. What should she do? Richard was in charge and he was dictating events, but every instinct in her was crying out against sending Connor home. True, it could be a simple virus, but if it wasn't…?

If only Nick was here. She respected him. He was the best A and E doctor she had ever met and he would surely know what to do for the best. But would he agree with Richard's judgement of the situation?

She turned away from Richard, giving herself time to

think. Thankfully he didn't stay to debate the issue, but moved on to see to another patient. He fully expected her to follow his orders.

Laura didn't stop to mull things over for long. She quickly fetched her medical supplies and then went to enlist Sarah's help.

Together they went back to Catherine and Connor. She discreetly drew the curtains to shield them from Richard.

By this time it was clear to see that Connor's condition was deteriorating. He lay back on the bed, his head cushioned by pillows. He was no longer taking much notice of what was going on, and when Laura examined him again, she discovered that his blood pressure was low while his heart rate was increasing.

'I'm going to give him an injection of penicillin,' she told Catherine, and his mother nodded acceptance.

Sarah made the little boy comfortable, and Catherine stroked her son's fair hair, soothing him while Laura proceeded with the injection.

'What do you think is wrong with him?' Catherine asked anxiously.

'I'm not certain yet, but I suspect that he might have a form of meningitis, and if it's bacterial rather than viral the penicillin will start to take effect. I need to do some tests so that I can be sure.'

Catherine went very pale all at once. 'Meningitis? That's bad, isn't it?' she said in a low voice. 'I thought vaccination provided immunity from that.'

'It gives protection from certain types,' Laura explained, 'but not from every kind.' She looked at her sister-in-law and saw that she was near to tears. 'Try not to get upset,' she said softly. 'As soon as I know what we're dealing with, I'll either continue with the antibiotic or start the treatment that will be most effective.'

She paused, and then added, 'I need to do a lumbar puncture now, Catherine. Sarah's going to help me to do that. Would you rather wait outside?'

'No.' Catherine shook her head fiercely. 'I want to stay here with him.'

'That's all right.' Laura set up the equipment for the lumbar puncture, and Sarah gently positioned Connor for the procedure.

'I'll send this sample to the laboratory for analysis,' she told Catherine when she withdrew the needle, 'but I'm not going to wait for the results before continuing treatment. I'm going set up an intravenous infusion so that we can give him fluids and a broad-spectrum antibiotic.'

She set to work to do that right away, while Sarah hurried off to the laboratory. As the nurse left the cubicle, Richard appeared. He looked grim, and Laura's heart sank.

'What's going on here?' he demanded. 'Haven't I told you to send this patient on his way?' He turned around and glared at Sarah's retreating form. 'And why have you thought it necessary to take up our nurse's valuable time like this?'

Sarah didn't stop, and Laura glanced quickly at Catherine. She didn't want her to witness an argument about the necessity of treating her son. She was already worried enough about what was happening to him.

She opened her mouth to speak, but Nick appeared at that moment in the periphery of her vision and said coolly, 'Dr Brett, Dr Caldwell—a moment, please.'

Laura flinched in shock. Nick's tone was firm and uncompromising. He must have heard Richard's angry rebuke, and now she was in trouble again. Her heart sank. How was she going to get out of it this time? This time it was deadly serious. Junior doctors did not flout the instructions of their superiors and get away with it.

Nick indicated that they should go over to where he stood, some short distance away. His brows were drawn together in an ominous black line, and her stomach knotted with tension.

'Dr Caldwell,' he said, taut-mouthed, 'is there some disagreement going on between you and Dr Brett?'

'There certainly is.' Dr Caldwell looked scathingly towards Laura. 'I have already seen that young patient and discharged him. I told Dr Brett to send him home, and I see no reason why she has chosen to ignore my instructions. It seems as though she has taken it upon herself to give her family privileged attention. Furthermore,' he added tersely, 'she appears to be subjecting the child to procedures which are, in my view, totally unnecessary. This is a complete waste of our time.'

Nick directed his gaze towards Laura. His eyes were dark and unfathomable, steadfastly fixed on her. 'Dr Brett? Do you have anything to say?'

She chose her words carefully. 'I accept that Dr Caldwell believes that my nephew is suffering from a simple viral infection, but my sister-in-law asked me to examine him, and after I had done that I considered that his condition merited further investigation. I take full responsibility for taking on his treatment now, and if it should turn out that I made the wrong treatment decision, I'm quite prepared to stand up to any criticism for my actions.'

Dr Caldwell's glance was scathing. 'I'm glad to hear

it, Dr Brett. I fully intend to put in a complaint about your behaviour.'

Dismayed, Laura stared at him. 'That's your prerogative, of course.' If he did that, her career was probably out of the window.

Nick was still frowning. 'You admit that you carried out procedures on the boy when you had been told to send him home?'

'I do.' She was shaking inside, but she pulled herself together and said, 'I acted in the best interests of the child. I thought I was doing what was right.'

Nick's eyes narrowed. 'What do you think is wrong with him?'

She pulled in a swift breath. 'I suspect that he might have a form of meningitis. These infections can take hold so rapidly that I didn't think I had any time to delay.'

'And you've started treatment already?'

She nodded. 'I thought it was for the best. His health was deteriorating. He had a bad headache and he was feverish. He was squinting, and when I shone a light in his eyes he turned away from it, so that I believe he was showing signs of photophobia. I accept that these signs could have been due to a viral infection, but I didn't want to take any risks.'

Nick nodded. 'In the circumstances, I think I would have done the same. No one wants to take any risks with a child's health. I would sooner answer to criticism after the event than to lose a patient through lack of action.'

He turned to Richard. 'I hope you agree that it's better to err on the side of caution? I don't think we can blame Dr Brett for doing what she thought was right. She was asked to give a second opinion, and she acted in the best interests of her patient. Whether or not a patient is a relative is immaterial.'

Richard ran a finger around his collar as though he was suddenly unbearably hot. 'Looking at it that way,' he said huffily, 'I suppose you have a point.'

Nick inclined his head briefly. 'Then we'll consider the matter closed, shall we?'

'I suppose so.'

'That's good.' He turned to Laura. 'Perhaps you'd like to go back to the boy and see how he's doing?'

She nodded and turned away immediately. As she went, she heard Nick say to Richard, 'Next time you have reason to find fault with a colleague, perhaps you'd have the decency to speak to them out of earshot of other people?'

Laura didn't catch Richard's mumbled reply. She went straight to Connor and found that he was slipping into unconsciousness. She called for help, and Sarah came to administer oxygen while Laura checked the dosage of the medication.

'What's happening?' Catherine said. 'Is he going to be all right?'

'We're doing everything that we can,' Laura assured her. 'It will take some time for his body to absorb the medication and for it to take effect. We'll admit him, of course. He will receive constant attention.'

She made arrangements for that to be done straight away, and Catherine went with Connor when he was taken to an isolation ward.

Laura watched them go, and felt as though her heart was breaking. He was only four years old. He was too young to be in this life-and-death situation. Suddenly, it was all too much for her. She needed to be alone, and she hurried to the doctors' lounge, where she could hide away from the rest of the world for a short time.

Nick found her there a few minutes later. She was in the far corner of the room, hidden away behind a screen, wiping away the tears that trickled down her cheeks.

'Laura, there you are. I wondered where you had got to.' His gaze travelled over her. 'You're worried about your nephew, aren't you?'

She nodded and tried to twist away as the tears threatened once more. He turned her around, drew her into his arms and gently stroked her hair, smoothing it into the nape of her neck.

'Lean on me,' he said softly. 'Cry it out, if that's what you want. It doesn't do to bottle it all up.'

'He's so tiny,' she said in a choked voice. 'How can this be happening? I love him so much, just as though he were mine.' She tried hard to get control of herself, but she wasn't succeeding very well. She dabbed at her eyes with a tissue. 'There's a bond between us, you know. It isn't just that he's my brother's son—it's something else that I can't put into words. Ever since he was born I've had a feeling that I can't describe, as though there's a link, a connection of some sort.'

She gulped down her tears and let out a shuddery breath. 'I know that I'm not explaining myself very well. It's something like *déjà vu*, if you like. I don't know what it is. All I know is that all my life I've felt as though something was missing…something from my childhood, maybe…someone I knew, perhaps…a childhood friend.' She shook her head. 'I'm confused. I don't know what I'm saying, and I know it sounds odd. I just couldn't bear to lose him.'

'You don't have to explain it,' he murmured. 'You're

doing everything that's possible to save him. No one can do any more.'

She looked up at him, still dabbing at her eyes with a tissue. 'I feel so helpless.'

'I know. There are times when we all feel that way. It's just a question of leaving the other doctors to do their job now, to support him through this. We have to stand back and wait, and sometimes that can be the hardest thing to do.' He trailed his thumb gently down her cheek. 'It's good that his mother brought him to you. She kept him here when she had been told to leave, because she knew that you would do everything that you could for him.'

'Have you seen him?'

He nodded. 'I went up to the ward to check on him. Catherine's going to stay with him. She's holding his hand and talking to him. Your brother's been informed, and he's on his way.'

She blinked in an effort to clear her vision and get herself back to normal. Nick's shirt was damp from her tears, and she reached up to touch the fine fabric. 'Look what I've done…I'm sorry. You must have better things to do than to try to comfort me.'

'You're the one who's important now,' he said softly. His arms were still around her, warm, solid and protective. He made her feel safe, as though he would keep out the outside world and anything that could harm her. 'Talk to me. Tell me what's on your mind. You were saying how you felt about Connor.'

She straightened up and looked into his eyes. They were such beautiful eyes, so full of compassion and sincerity. He was a good man, a man that you could rely on in times of trouble, a man who would be a bedrock, a foundation of security, if ever it was needed.

'I don't think I can. I'm too confused.'

He smiled. 'That's only to be expected.' He became thoughtful. 'Do you think that when you see Connor it makes you think about what it might be like to have a child of your own?'

Laura shook her head. 'No, that isn't it. I'm too unsettled to even think about that just now. There were all those years of medical training, and now I'm only just finding my feet in A and E.'

'And you've fairly recently moved back home to be near to your father,' he said musingly. 'There have been a lot of changes going on in your life, haven't there? You were away for some time, and I imagine that must have made you feel a little homesick. Is that part of the problem?'

'What do you mean?'

'Has it ever occurred to you that your feelings about Connor might stem from your own vulnerability, from the fact that you were adopted as a small child? Perhaps something inside you identifies with a time when you felt that you were lost and alone among strangers.'

'I never thought about it that way.' She frowned. 'You could be right, I suppose.'

'Did you talk to your father about what happened when you we're young, about what led to you being adopted?'

'Yes, we did have a conversation, although I already knew some of what he said.' She was quiet for a moment. 'My parents were separated, I think. When I was two years old, my natural mother brought me into hospital. I was suffering from the same condition as Connor—meningitis. My dad, my adoptive father, was a young hospital doctor at the time, and he became responsible for my care when I was admitted.'

She moistened her lips with the tip of her tongue. 'Apparently, one day, my natural mother left the hospital to go and get a change of clothes, and when she was driving back to me she was involved in a car crash. She was badly injured, and she lapsed into a coma. Her injuries were very severe and it took a long, long time for her to recover.'

'Do you remember any of it? When you recovered from your own illness, I mean.'

She shook her head. 'Not really. I was only in hospital for a few weeks, but my dad said he became very fond of me during that time. He offered to give me a foster-home while my mother was ill.'

'Why couldn't your real father take care of you?'

'As far as I know, he disappeared when he separated from my mother. Nobody could find him and there was some talk that he had gone overseas and changed his name. I heard later, years later, that he had died in a skiing accident.'

Nick's expression was serious. 'So you were fostered. What happened after that? Didn't your mother get well again?'

She nodded. 'It was a matter of a couple of years before she recovered enough to come out of rehabilitation, but it appeared that as a result of the accident she had lost her memory. She didn't know me at all. There were visits, so I'm told, but by that time I had settled into my new home and I resisted all efforts to go with my mother. In the end, she agreed to let me be adopted.'

'That must have been a difficult decision for her to make.'

'I imagine so, though she never did get her memory back, and after a while the visits stopped because the adoption authorities thought that they were too upsetting for me.'

She made a face. 'I thought I was going to be taken away from the home where I felt safe—or so they told me. I think that's the reason my father didn't talk to me very much about what had happened. He also didn't want to upset my adoptive mother. She was finding the situation difficult to cope with, too. She had looked after me for more than two years, and I was part of the family. She told me later that she couldn't bear the thought of me being taken away from her.'

She pulled in a shaky breath. 'As time went on, I suppose I could have tried to get in touch with my real mother, but it would have stirred everything up again. My dad didn't want me to go in search of her and discover that she still had no maternal feelings for me or even a recollection that she had given birth to me.'

'I'm sorry. That's a tragic story.' He looked at her intently. 'Do you think that perhaps now is the time for you to lay the ghost? Perhaps that's what's been at the back of your mind all this time.'

'You mean that I should go and find her?'

He nodded. 'I think it might be a good idea.'

'I'm not sure that my father would be happy about that. I think he might still have reservations about it.'

'But this isn't about your father, is it? It's about you. You're upset, and it isn't just that Connor is ill. You said yourself that you're all mixed up about what went on in your childhood, and that you feel something is missing. This is the second time that you've been unhappy and overwrought at work, and I think you'll go on being emotionally drained until you sort out what happened. Perhaps the only way that you'll be able to do that is to go and look for your real mother.'

'I don't know. I'm not sure.' It wouldn't bother Nick if her father was upset. The two of them were always at loggerheads over something or other, so why would he care?

She realised with a small sense of shock that she was still in Nick's arms. Easing back a little, she tried to carefully edge away from him, and he let her go.

She said slowly, 'I didn't thank you for defending me back there, when Richard and I had a disagreement. It was scary for a while. I thought I might be out of a job fairly soon.'

'He's a conceited, arrogant man, full of his own importance, but he's only here as a locum. He won't be around for much longer.'

'Won't he?'

'I think it's unlikely. I've accepted the post of consultant here, and they're appointing a new specialist registrar. I think we'll be up to speed fairly soon, and we'll have the department in good order again.'

Her eyes widened. 'You've accepted?' She was silent for a moment, thinking about that, and then she said, 'I'm glad for you.'

He gave a wry smile. 'But you have your reservations about it, don't you? That's understandable, I suppose. There's no going back, though, and it's just something you have to get used to.' He looked at her, and it was as though he read her mind. 'Your father, too.'

CHAPTER FIVE

CONNOR was still in a critical condition when Laura looked in on him a few days later. He looked pale and intensely fragile, hooked up to tubes and drips and linked to monitors that bleeped quietly in the background.

Her father was sitting by his bedside, and he hardly turned from his vigil when she entered the room. He looked haggard, she thought. He must be distraught to see his grandson looking so vulnerable, and she wanted to reach out and comfort him.

'It's been such a shock to all of us, seeing this happen to Connor,' she murmured. 'He went downhill so rapidly. It was frightening to see.' She pressed her lips together as though it might alleviate some of the anguish. 'I come up here and look in on him every chance I have, but there's been no change for some time. It's awful, isn't it, being able to do nothing but wait and hope that the swelling around his brain will subside in time?'

'It's something you dread, the thought that it can happen to one of your own.' He looked up at her. 'I'm just thankful that you were the one who treated him, that you recognised the signs. I can't bear to imagine what might have happened if Catherine had taken him home.'

He shook his head. 'She and Matthew have been at his bedside almost every minute, and they look dreadful. I managed to persuade them to go and get something to eat before they become ill themselves. They don't seem to be coping too well, and there's nothing I can say or do to reassure them. We just have to keep praying that he'll come through this.'

She laid a hand on his shoulder. 'Up to now he's always been a sturdy little boy. He must be able to put up a fight…he must.'

Her father was silent for a moment. 'I remember watching you when you were tiny, and ill like this. You looked so frail, and it was touch and go for a time whether you would pull through, but you confounded us all. You had such a strong fighting spirit. I hope Connor has that trait in him.'

'Matthew's always been a fighter. I've never known him to give in to anything, so Connor must have inherited some of that.'

'Let's hope so,' he said, grim-faced. He sighed. 'I should get back to work. The paperwork is still piling up.'

'Me, too. At least we're close by. Sarah's promised that she'll bring me any news as soon as she has it, but I have to keep checking up on him for myself.'

They walked back towards A and E together a few minutes later. 'How do you feel about Nick's appointment as consultant?' she asked. 'Is it going to be a problem for you?'

'It's more than likely. Some of his plans could spell trouble, but there's nothing I can do to turn back the clock. Management made their decision knowing full well that he had a far-sighted vision for the future. They were very impressed with him, and very taken with his ideas.'

'Will that mean a lot of upheaval for the department?'

'I'm sure it will. It goes without saying that what he wants will take a great deal of money, and usually these things can end up meaning that we have to undergo more cost-cutting measures.' His mouth made a grim line. 'I don't suppose that will bother Nick. He'll go ahead with his plans regardless of how they might affect other people.'

'But it will be some time before anything happens, won't it?'

'Not necessarily. He's already asked that a second consultant be appointed. He's concerned that there isn't adequate cover for evenings and weekends and that, as a result, patients are being left vulnerable. Management has agreed to that request because patient numbers have been growing for some time now, but it will be a while before an appointment can be made, and I'm not sure that Nick will be satisfied with that. I've done my best to suggest strategies for the interim.'

His mouth twisted. 'As to everything else that Nick has in mind, I'm certain that he'll want to put his ideas into place as soon as possible. He doesn't believe in letting the grass grow under his feet.'

Laura looked at her father anxiously. 'And all that will affect you, personally, won't it? Is it going to mean a lot more disagreements between the two of you?'

'I'm sure that it will, one way or another, especially if I have to administer the changes he wants. I set the department up in its present form, and he'll probably tear it apart.'

'I'm so sorry.'

'It can't be helped. Besides, at the moment he's being remarkably restrained in his dealings with me. I expect he realises that you and I are under a good deal of strain just now.'

'That's something, at any rate,' she murmured, though she wasn't altogether convinced. Watching Nick move into prime position in charge of A and E was a bit like waiting for a rumbling volcano to erupt.

The concern that he had shown for her the other day had been unexpected, and unsettling. He had been supportive and comforting, and she had been glad of his strength and protective gestures. It had made her feel warm and fuzzy and she wasn't sure that was a good thing. Being aware of him as a man, and as an all too attractive one at that, could be altogether too disturbing…especially now that he was her boss.

He was at work in A and E when she arrived there a few minutes later. 'We've a suspected overdose patient coming in,' one of the nurses told her. 'Should be here any time now.'

They could hear the ambulance siren already, and Laura hurried to the patient as he was brought in. He was a man in his late thirties, and it was clear that he was in pain.

She was aware of Nick in the background, busy treating a patient but still closely observing everything that she did and taking a keen interest as she spoke to the paramedics.

'He's been taking paracetamol for the last day or so,' the paramedic told her. 'He had a bad toothache, according to his wife, and didn't want to go to the dentist. He started with a small dose, but it didn't do anything for the pain so he increased the tablets last night and this morning. She found him keeled over in the bathroom and called us. He's been vomiting.'

'How many tablets has he taken, do you know?' Laura asked.

'There are two empty packets, so his wife reckons around thirty-two. He's been washing them down with alcohol, apparently.'

'That's a lot of paracetamol in a short space of time,' Laura said worriedly. 'We'll do a blood test right away to determine the paracetamol level,' she told the nurse, 'and we'll do urine tests as well. We'll monitor his blood glucose hourly.'

'Are you going to do a stomach wash-out?' the nurse asked.

'Yes, and we'll begin his medication as soon as possible.'

'Will you be giving him methionine?'

Laura shook her head. 'No. If he vomits again, we can't be sure that it will be absorbed. We'll start an infusion of N-acetylcysteine in dextrose to see if we can prevent any liver damage.'

She was worried about her patient, and at the same time she was anxious because Nick was watching her. This was a potential life or death situation, and she wondered if he doubted her capabilities.

She examined her patient, and discovered that there was tenderness in his abdomen, over his liver.

'What are his chances, do you think?' the nurse asked in a low voice, some time later.

'It's hard to say at the moment,' Laura answered. 'If it's less than sixteen hours since he took the majority of the tablets, then he might just be lucky. The blood tests aren't back yet, but I can't delay in giving him the antidote.'

She made arrangements to admit him, and then went to speak to his wife, who was in the waiting room.

'How is he doing?' Nick asked, when she returned.

'He's not too well at the moment.' She frowned, wondering whether he thought she had been remiss in some way. 'Should I be doing anything else?'

'There's very little you can do, but if he shows signs

of liver failure you should consult the transplant people. That will be his only salvation.' He gave her a considering glance. 'You're wondering why I'm asking, aren't you? I'm not suggesting that you can't cope on your own. I'm responsible for the doctors on my team—I'm just making sure that you know that I'm here and I'm available to help you if I'm needed.'

'Thank you. I'll bear that in mind.' He had only been officially in charge for a few days, but already he was making his presence felt, she acknowledged ruefully. She had been very much aware that he had been in control when Tom had been taken ill, but now his decisions would be paramount. It made her nervous, just thinking about it.

At the end of her shift she went back to the ward where Connor was being cared for to see if there was any change in him.

'He's still the same,' Matthew said, looking wretched. 'He hasn't moved or opened his eyes.'

Laura checked his charts. 'At least he's holding his own, and there's been no change for the worse. That has to be good news.' She was trying her utmost to be positive, to look on the bright side, but it was very difficult.

She stayed for a few minutes, looking at her sweet-faced nephew, stroking his silky hair and praying that he would have the strength to get well.

Nick was outside in the corridor as she left the ward. He was talking to a paediatric consultant. He was leaning negligently against the wall, his long legs crossed at the ankles, and Laura couldn't help but notice what a striking figure he made. He was tall and lean, his long body emphasised by the immaculately tailored dark grey suit that he wore. In profile, his jaw was strong and clean cut. It was disturbing, being so constantly aware of him.

As Laura came towards him he straightened up and the paediatric consultant went on his way.

'You've been to see your nephew?' His eyes darkened as he watched her expression. 'How is he?'

'There's been no change.'

'I'm sorry. This must be difficult for all of you.'

She nodded but said nothing, and he turned to walk with her back along the corridor. As they passed by one of the glass-walled paediatric wards, Laura heard the sound of children squabbling and glanced in at them to see what was going on. Two infants, who were both a little younger than Connor, she guessed, were engaged in a tug of war over a toy truck, and she stood for a moment, watching them. Their childish voices were raised as each fought for possession.

She frowned, a strange sensation rippling through her, and for a moment she felt dizzy and out of sync with everything that was going on. She put a hand out, resting it palm flat on the glass, in an effort to steady herself.

'Are you all right?' Nick asked.

She dragged her gaze from the children and stared up at him. 'I think so… I was a little light-headed for a moment, but I'm not really sure what happened.'

His brow furrowed, and she made an effort to explain herself better. 'I was looking at the children, and then I had this odd sensation run through me, almost like a flash of memory.'

She gave a peculiar little grimace. 'I know it sounds silly, and I can't describe it properly. It's happened to me a few times just lately, and mostly it's when I'm around small children. It's very strange and I don't understand it at all. I don't know why it keeps happening to me.'

'You can probably put it down to the worry over

Connor. It's bound to affect you in one way or another. Or the dizziness could simply be the result of a lack of food. Have you eaten yet?'

She frowned, and then she shook her head. 'I didn't have time. I was going to grab something to eat, but then the man who had taken the overdose was brought in. After that we were rushed off our feet with people coming in with minor injuries.'

'Then we ought to get some food inside you as soon as possible. You've finished for the day, haven't you? What do you say? We could go and get some supper right now. We could go to the Swan. It's close by and they do a good meal. I wanted to talk to you anyway— I have a few ideas I'd like to sound out with you about the department.'

She could hardly refuse now that he had suggested that they talk about his plans. Any changes he made in the department could affect her father, and she wanted to know first hand what he had in mind.

'All right. That sounds like a good idea.'

The Swan was a local pub that was commonly frequented by staff from the hospital. It was comfortably furnished, with upholstered seating set out in little recessed alcoves, which were separated by decorative wood and glass screens. The food was always of a good standard, and there was a warm atmosphere where people could relax away from the concerns of their everyday work.

Nick ordered their meals and brought drinks to their table. Laura sipped at hers and said, 'What was it that you wanted to talk to me about? My father mentioned to me that you had a number of ideas you wanted to try out.'

'That's true. First and foremost, I think we need another consultant for A and E so that our patients aren't left vulnerable at evenings and weekends. With the best will in the world I can't spread myself all ways. I'm not sure how long it will take before an appointment is made, but in the meantime we have to work out how we can manage things.'

'My father said that he had suggested alternatives to you.'

He nodded. 'He suggested that we appoint specialist emergency nurses to provide cover.'

Laura considered that. 'That sounds sensible, don't you agree?'

'I do. I'm just concerned that they might need extra help, expert advice in situations that are beyond their training.'

'That can be provided, I would imagine. Some hospitals are using video links so that nurses can call on specialists in their area to give them advice when it's needed.'

He nodded thoughtfully. 'We could try that. It might work.'

A waitress brought their food to the table, and Laura suddenly realised how hungry she was. She tucked into her lasagne with relish, and watched Nick eat his mixed grill with equal enjoyment. He talked to her about his experience with other A and E departments, and she realised how hard he must have worked over the last few years. It didn't surprise her that he had reached the level of consultant while he was still in his mid-thirties.

'Would you like a dessert?' he asked.

'I think I would,' she said, 'though I'm not sure that my waistline would agree.'

His glance slanted over her, moving smoothly over her curves and leaving a trail of warmth in its wake.

When he looked up again, there was wry amusement in his blue eyes. 'I don't think you have any need to worry on that score,' he said softly. 'From what I've seen, you're in perfect shape.'

She felt a flush of heat streak along her cheekbones, and she resisted the urge to run a defensive hand over her snugly fitting skirt in order to hide her long, shapely legs from his view. She was comfortable wearing cotton tops that fitted like a second skin, and when she was at work she preferred to dress in skirts that finished around knee length. Now, though, his attention was making her self-conscious.

'I like to keep fit,' she mumbled. 'Whenever I get the chance, I go swimming, or sometimes I like to walk along the mountain paths and take in the scenery. It's so beautiful around here, don't you think?' She hoped he would accept a change of topic.

'I certainly do,' he said, but his gaze was still fixed steadily on her features and she felt a ripple of awareness run through her entire body.

He ordered their desserts, and then to her relief he talked to her about the mountain walks thereabouts and the scenic areas that they both liked to explore.

Her mobile phone bleeped a few minutes later as she was enjoying her chocolate dessert, and she put down her spoon so that she could check her messages. When she looked up again, she found that Nick was studying her intently.

'Is there news of Connor?'

She shook her head. 'No, not yet. My brother wants me to pass on a message to my father, that's all. He probably can't reach him just now because he'll be on his way home. It's nothing important. He'll want talk to my father about Connor's condition, and glean any expert advice available. It's understandable. Neither he nor Catherine knows which way to turn. It was a shock to them when Richard tried to send Connor home, and I think it's added to their worry. They're afraid that even a slight delay in starting treatment could have caused him to be even more sick.'

'I can understand how they must be feeling.' He called a waitress over and ordered coffees.

'That's one of the reasons that I want to get an emergency paediatric unit up and running,' he said, as he finished his dessert a moment later. 'Children will be directed straight to that unit, where we'll have paediatric specialists to attend to them right away. I think parents might feel a lot happier about the way their children are being cared for. That should help to allay a lot of fears, both in parents and children. There would be no waiting around in adult surroundings that can be frightening for children. We would make the area especially pleasant, the whole place decorated and geared up for paediatric patients.'

'You've thought this all through, haven't you?'

'I have. I'd also like to have a play area for the not so badly injured. If there are toys available, or activities that they can enjoy, I think children will be less fretful and easier to treat in the end.'

'I've seen that work in some hospitals,' Laura said carefully. 'But usually there is a play supervisor on hand. All the things that you're suggesting will cost a great deal of money. Do you think that you're likely to get what you want?'

'I'm pretty certain of it.'

'But that will mean cost-cutting measures, won't it? My father certainly believes so, and I'm sure he's right.

I can't see that any of this will come about without procedures being put in place to streamline everything else.'

He shrugged. 'I dare say that it will, but probably those measures will make things more efficient in the long run. Your father has worked in the hospital for a long time and he knows what goes on and what could help to make things work better.' He hesitated, and then said, 'You're probably in the best position to talk him through it, and make him see that change is not necessarily a bad thing.'

She sent him a bleak glance. Was this why he had asked her out this evening…because he wanted her to work on her father and bring him around to his way of thinking?

'Perhaps he can foresee some of the effects that change will have on people's lives. How many of them are going to be drawn into new methods of working, or discover that their rotas are different, or even find that their role within the department has changed because of what you decide to implement? You don't much care what will happen to other people, how they might be affected, as long as your plans are carried out, do you?' she said.

'Let's wait and see what happens, shall we? There's no point laying obstacles down before we even make a start.' His eyes narrowed on her. 'I know what's behind this. You're concerned about your father, and that's understandable, but don't you think you ought be taking care of yourself? You have problems of your own that you need to deal with.'

Her gaze homed in on him. 'Do I?'

'You know that you do. We've talked about this before, about the fact that it might be a good idea for you to try to find out what has happened to your natural mother. A lot of the insecurities I sense in you stem from the fact that you don't know very much about her. There must be a lot of questions going around in your head all the time, and until they're answered you won't be able to get your life in gear. You've pushed it to the back of your mind for long enough. It's time you got on and did something about it.'

'I'm perfectly capable of deciding what I need to do with my life,' she said sharply. 'I don't need you to be telling me what I ought or ought not to be doing.'

'I'm not sure that's true. You say you're having these problems, flashes of memory, and it could be that you're thinking about your childhood. You can't come to terms with this great hole in your life, and I don't think you'll be able to function properly as a complete and rounded person until you confront your past.'

'I'm not sure that I can do that, especially now when my father is so anxious about what's happening to Connor. I don't want to give him anything else to worry about.'

'None of this is going change the outcome where Connor is concerned, is it? And I'm sure your father can take care of himself.'

Her green eyes sparked. 'You don't care how he might feel about any of this, do you? You've no consideration for him at all.'

'I'm just telling you how it is. Your father has his life, and you have yours. There comes a time when you have to be true to yourself and not worry so much about other people.'

'I'll think it over,' she said. She swallowed the last of her coffee and set her cup down. 'I think it's time I started for home. If there's any news about Connor, I

want to be ready. My brother and his wife might
need me.'

'Of course. I'll see you to your car.'

They didn't talk any more about controversial sub-
jects, and when she slid into her car a few minutes later,
he stood and watched as she started up the engine. She
didn't look back, but even so she was conscious of his
gaze following her as she drove away.

Why had he asked her out this evening? Was it as
he'd said, that he'd wanted to sound her out about his
ideas for the department? Or had he had an ulterior mo-
tive? He made it seem as though he cared for her, as
though he had her interests at heart, but perhaps there
was more to it than that. Perhaps he was more concerned
about the influence she might have on her father to
smooth his path.

CHAPTER SIX

'THERE you are, sweetheart,' Laura said gently, as she finished binding the little girl's ankle. The child was about three years old and it was clear that she had been overwhelmed by her experience of A and E. She peeped out at Laura from under her lashes, and Laura gave her an encouraging smile. 'Does that feel a bit more comfortable?'

The girl stuck her thumb in her mouth and nodded shyly.

'Good, I'm glad about that.' Laura gave her a smiley face sticker for her T-shirt.

Turning to the girl's mother, Laura said, 'You can give her infant paracetamol to ease the pain, if you like. I think she'll be fine in a few days' time.'

'Thank you.' The woman led her little girl away, and Laura left the cubicle and went over to the desk where her father was talking to Nick.

Her father was shaking his head and looking grim, and she wondered whether they were in the middle of yet another heated discussion. She approached them both warily.

'Is something wrong here? You both look as though you could do with some time to cool down.'

Nick's brows met in a dark line. 'I was just telling David that work on the paediatric area will be starting next week. The workmen have been doing repairs to the old hospital block next to this one for some time now, and they're almost finished. As soon as the supplies are delivered, they'll start work on turning it into an emergency paediatric unit.'

'Their presence is affecting work in several departments,' her father put in, 'and I've had numerous complaints. Their equipment is blocking corridors and getting in everybody's way. I've spoken to them several times about it already.'

'I appreciate that it's a nuisance, but you can't have change without some disruption,' Nick said dismissively. 'It won't go on for ever. We'll get the painters in as soon as possible, and then I've someone lined up who can come in and finish it off with murals of cartoon characters and pictures of toys. We've even worked out a theme for the ceiling.'

'I'm sure it will be a wonderful project,' Laura said in an even tone. She glanced quickly at her father, and then back at Nick. 'It will be a shame to see the paediatric cubicles go from here, though. My father put in a lot of work to make this area suitable for the assessment and treatment of children, and we've all become used to this being the tots area. He was hoping that we would be able to extend it.'

'I know. But the new unit will give us a much larger area and we'll be able to treat more patients there than we can at present. The whole ethos of A and E now is to move patients through the system as quickly as possible, and that should help.'

'What will happen to those children who are brought in for treatment at the same time as their injured parents?' her father put in. 'The way it is now, they can often be treated alongside their parents and the parents can offer reassurance of some sort.'

'There's no reason that can't still be an option,' Nick countered. 'We'll do whatever we can to keep families happy. We can find ways to work around these situations.'

'I hope so,' her father said. Laura could see that he wasn't convinced. He went along with the idea of a new unit, but she knew that it was disheartening for him to see his work being dismantled bit by bit.

'We'll have everything up and running within a few weeks, hopefully,' Nick said. He looked at Laura's father, his mouth firming. 'It's called progress.'

Laura grimaced and reached for her next patient's file. Trying to keep the peace between them was becoming more difficult by the day, and she wished that it didn't have to come down to a struggle between an energetic young consultant and an eminent administrator who was nearing retirement. It was such an uneven contest, and she had no doubt who would win in the end.

She went back to work, and she was in the middle of treating a man with a broken finger when Sarah looked in on her.

'Do you have a minute?' she asked. 'Can I speak to you outside?'

'Yes, of course.' She turned to her patient and said, 'Will you excuse me? I'll send someone in to strap up your fingers and organise a prescription for painkillers.'

Outside the cubicle, she arranged for a nurse to finish off, and went with Sarah to the desk. 'What is it?' she asked. 'Do we have a major incident coming in?'

Sarah shook her head. 'No, it's nothing like that. It's Connor. He's awake. I thought you would like to know.'

'Awake? Oh, I've been waiting to hear that for so long. My nerves have been in shreds.'

'I know. That's why I came to tell you straight away.'

'What sort of state is he in, do you know?' Meningitis

could play havoc with a child's well-being in all sorts of ways. 'Is his hearing intact? Are there any residual problems?'

'I'm afraid I don't know. Why don't you go and see him? I'm sure Nick will let you slip away for half an hour.'

'I'll go and ask him right now.'

She hurried away, and collared Nick as he was attending to a patient with a pneumothorax.

'Nick, I've just heard that Connor is stirring. Is it all right if I go and spend some time with him?'

'Yes…you go. We're not too busy down here. I'll bleep you if anything major comes in.'

'Thanks.' She shot off without stopping to look back.

'He woke up and asked for his teddy bear,' the staff nurse told her when she arrived at the ward. 'Well…his mum and dad first, and then his teddy bear. He hasn't said much else since then, but we're pleased that he's responsive.'

Laura felt a rush of relief. 'Oh, I'm so happy to hear that news. I can't tell you how much I've been on edge these last few days.'

'I can imagine. Catherine's with him, and she's expecting Matthew to join her in a little while, but you can go in for a few minutes. We don't want to tire him out, mind.'

'I'll be careful, I promise.'

Connor was holding on tightly to his teddy bear when she went along to his bedside. Catherine held his hand as though any small contact with her son was like precious lifeblood to her.

Laura watched them and wondered how her own mother must have felt when her child had been brought into hospital. Had she felt as Catherine had, full of love and need, desperate for any small sign that her child was going to be all right?

Catherine turned and gave Laura a brilliant smile. 'Isn't it wonderful? I'm just so happy that he's back with us.' She turned to her son. 'I love you so much, baby…you know that, don't you?'

Connor didn't answer her, but his eyes opened wider and he looked at his mother as though everything was a little strange in his world. Then he turned his head to look at Laura, before slowly closing his eyes again.

'Is he all right?' Catherine asked anxiously.

Laura nodded. 'I think so. He's probably still weak after everything that he's been through. Try not to worry. Just stay with him and be there to reassure him when he wakes up again. He should start to get stronger every day now.'

She stayed for a while longer until Matthew arrived, and then she slipped away.

Nick sent her a questioning look as soon as she returned to A and E. 'How is he?'

'Still very weak, but at least he's taking note of some of the things around him.'

'It's early days yet. You just have to be patient.'

'I know, but it isn't easy.'

Sarah interrupted them, saying in a brisk tone, 'The paramedics are bringing two patients in. There was a road accident, a collision between a car and a young man on a motorbike. They're not sure about the full extent of the biker's injuries, but he's in a pretty bad way. The car driver slammed into a wall when she tried to avoid the biker, and she's suffering from cuts and whiplash injuries as far as they can tell. The paramedics are querying whether she might have spinal injuries.'

'OK, people. Let's make sure that we are ready for

them.' Nick was already on the move, calling down to X-Ray to warn the radiologist to prepare for injured patients. 'I'll take the car driver,' he said. 'Laura, will you take the biker?'

She nodded, and as soon as her patient was brought in she began to examine him. James Carson was eighteen years old, and it was the first time he had been out on a motorbike, apparently.

'There's bruising and tenderness of the abdomen,' she murmured to the nurse who was helping. 'I suspect he has an internal injury, and that he's haemorrhaging. We'll need an X-ray to check for fractured ribs, and also an abdominal film. Let's get some blood for cross-matching, too.'

Nick was busy with his patient, but he looked across to where she was working and said, 'What are you dealing with?'

'I suspect that he may have a ruptured spleen,' she told him. 'I'm starting an intravenous infusion to replace lost fluids and to give him pain relief.'

He nodded. 'You'd better call for a surgical consultation. If it is a ruptured spleen he will need to go to Theatre as soon as possible.'

'I'll do that.'

By the time the X-rays were available, the surgical consultant was on hand. 'Looks like a ruptured spleen to me,' he said, studying the films. 'I'll have to remove it. Do we have the parents' consent?'

'Yes, we do. I'll go and have a word with them.'

James's parents were in a terrible state, she discovered. They were bickering over the fact that the motorbike had been a birthday present for their son.

'I never wanted him to have a bike,' the mother was saying. 'This is all your fault, for encouraging him.'

The father looked up anxiously as Laura entered the room. 'How is he? Is there any news?'

'We're going to take him up to Theatre right away,' she told him. 'It looks as though his spleen was damaged when he was in collision with the car, and the injury was made worse because his ribs fractured and then punctured the organ. The surgeon will remove it.'

'Why does he have to do that?' the mother asked. 'Can't he repair the damage?'

'I'm afraid that's not possible,' Laura said. 'In fact, James should be able to cope reasonably well without his spleen. Usually, if the spleen is removed, its function is largely taken over by parts of the lymphatic system and the liver. He should be able to lead a normal life afterwards, but the surgeon will talk to you about that.'

She looked from one to the other. 'You're in for a bit of a wait, I'm afraid. Can we get you anything? Tea or coffee? There's a cafeteria if you would prefer to wait in there.'

They both shook their heads. 'We're all right, thank you,' James's father said. 'We'll wait here, if that's all right with you.'

'That's fine. Someone will come and talk to you as soon as we have any more news.'

She hurried back to A and E to see if Nick needed any help. He was studying the X-rays.

'How is your patient doing?' Laura asked.

The woman didn't look to be in very good shape. Her neck was supported by a rigid brace to prevent any further damage from occurring. Her eyes were wide with fear, despite Nick's attempts to reassure her. She was clearly terrified of the condition she found herself in.

'I can't feel my arms or legs,' she whispered.

A nurse leaned over to offer her comfort. 'Try to relax,' she told her. 'We're waiting for the test results. As soon as we know anything, we'll tell you.'

'The X-ray film shows a slight fracture of one of the neck vertebrae,' Nick murmured. 'That in itself is serious but, provided we keep her neck immobile, that could heal. I'm waiting for the results of the MRI scan. She's showing signs of spinal injury, but that may just be due to swelling of the cord at the moment.'

'Poor woman. Let's hope the cord is intact.'

She tried to keep her voice level, but she couldn't disguise a slight tremor, and Nick gave her a quick glance. 'What's wrong?'

She shook her head, not wanting to say what was on her mind, but Nick was too astute for that to make any difference.

'Are you thinking about your mother?'

'About my natural mother, yes.' She pressed her lips together. It was happening to her more and more these days, this feeling that the past was part of the present. 'She must have suffered some kind of spinal injury if it took her such a long time to recover. I can't imagine what she must have gone through. It was bad enough being injured, but then to be told that she had a child as well—it must have been doubly difficult for her.'

'Perhaps it wasn't quite so bad if she didn't remember the child.'

'I'll never know, will I, unless I try to find her and talk to her about it?'

He looked at her, his eyes serious as he searched her face. 'She may still not remember.'

'I know, but you've been right all along. I have to find out.' She straightened her shoulders. 'I think I'll make a start on looking for her next week. My shift starts later then, so I'll have the mornings free to do whatever's necessary.'

'Would you like me to help? I'm on the later shift, too, so I could go along with you to the adoption registry, just to give you my support, if you like.'

She shook her head. 'No, thank you. I'll manage.'

'Are you sure? You might find this whole business more difficult than you anticipate.'

'Even so...'

'You might have some trouble finding out where she lives. After all this time she might have moved house, but I'm fairly well acquainted with the local area and the counties round about. I can help you.'

'I'll be all right. This is something I need to do on my own.'

He frowned, his eyes darkening, and she knew that he wasn't happy with her answer. Did he think that she was pushing him away? She was, of course, but there was nothing she could do about that. It was thoughtful of him to offer to help, but she didn't think she could cope with sharing too much of this with him. It had been hard for her to get this far, and she still had doubts about whether she was doing the right thing. This was something very personal, intensely private, and she needed to do it by herself. That way, if it all went wrong, she wouldn't have dragged anyone else along with her.

She thought about telling her father what she was planning to do, but when she went to his office later that day, she found him looking anxiously at the paperwork on his desk.

'More worries?' she asked.

'The hospital budget,' he said flatly. 'It looks as though we're going to be looking at job cuts sooner or later.'

She was shocked. 'Job cuts? Is it definite?'

'It's probable.'

'But why… I mean, how will it be decided who stays and who goes?'

'That's not clear yet, but mostly they will look for cuts in administrative positions. I expect people might be asked to take early retirement.' He grimaced. 'People like me.'

'But if you don't want to retire, what will happen then?' Her father didn't want to leave, she knew that. He had several years left before he needed to retire, and he had always said that there was work he wanted to finish, procedures he wanted to see put in place.

'If it comes to that, if people don't agree to go, then I suppose redundancy could be forced on them.'

'I'm so sorry.' She didn't know what she could say or do that would ease the situation. She felt wretched for him, and then she started to feel anger start up inside. This was Nick's doing, wasn't it? He had pushed for change, and now her father might be the one to suffer the consequences.

She stayed and talked to her father for a while longer, but she didn't have the heart to tell him that she was thinking of looking for her natural mother. How could she, when he had other problems on his mind? Besides, her search might come to nothing, and what was the point of upsetting him if that was going to be the case?

Before she did anything, she had to be clear in her mind that Connor was all right. She visited him over the next few days, and each day he looked a little stronger.

This morning, he was sitting up in bed, and she sat beside him so that they could do some jigsaws together. He concentrated hard as they tried to fit the pieces into place.

'It's a doggy,' Connor said with a chuckle as the picture formed. 'He's got a flower on his head. He's silly!'

'He does look funny, doesn't he?' Laura said, laughing with him. She looked at him, happy to see that the colour was returning to his cheeks.

Satisfied that he was well on the road to recovery, she left him a while later and set off for the office that kept the records of adoptions.

'You say your mother's surname was Somerville?' the man behind the desk queried. He flicked through a ledger, and after a while he nodded thoughtfully, his brows lifting. 'Here we are. It seems that you're in luck. She left details so that she could be contacted.' He frowned. 'This is the last known address I have for her. It looks as though it belongs to this county, so it shouldn't take you too long to track it down.'

He wrote the address down on a piece of paper and handed it to her. 'I hope that you're successful.'

'Thank you.' Laura tucked the piece of paper into her bag and hurried out into the street. Her heart was thumping so hard that she could feel it in her throat. It had been so simple. All she had to do was to find the house where her mother lived. There was no time to do it right now, but she would set out tomorrow before work.

Would she simply go and knock on the front door? There was no phone number, so she couldn't make contact that way. Anyway, after all this time, she couldn't bear to wait for much longer, and she didn't want to risk sending a letter. Something could go wrong, and she wanted to find out as soon as possible if her mother was really there.

Next morning, though, her nerves were getting the better of her. Was she doing the right thing? She drove to her mother's last known address, but as soon as she reached it, she knew that something was wrong. The housing estate that had existed all those years ago was no longer there. Instead, she found that it had been re-developed into a shopping parade and a children's play area.

She felt numb inside. All her hopes had been dashed in one swift blow and she didn't know what she was going to do now.

Her shift was due to start in an hour, and she drove to the hospital in a daze. She parked the car in her usual spot and then began to walk towards the main building, still mulling things over in her mind.

A service road crossed in front of the building, and Laura walked towards the crossing point, following a young mother and her two infants. 'Come on, Anne-Marie,' the mother was saying. 'I wish you would stop dawdling. Robert's appointment is in five minutes' time and we must hurry up or we'll be late.' The little boy tugged at his mother's arm and she turned to him, lean-ing down to hear what he was saying.

The little girl wasn't taking any notice of either of them. She began to walk along the kerb edge, trying to balance like a gymnast, and all at once she lost her foot-ing and began to tumble into the path of an oncoming car. Her mother screamed. 'Anne-Marie, no…'

Laura rushed forward and bent down to grab hold of the little girl, pushing her back towards the pavement. She heard a screech of car tyres and the squeal of brakes, and then she felt a thud as the car hit her shoulder and the impact knocked her to the ground.

Laura lay in the road for a moment, wondering if the little girl was safe. Then she slowly moved to a sitting position and saw that Anne-Marie was standing on the pavement with her mother and brother, looking shaken but unharmed, and she felt an overwhelming sense of relief flood through her.

'I'm so sorry,' a man's voice said. 'Are you badly hurt? It all happened so quickly. She fell in front of me and I tried to stop but there wasn't time.'

She looked up and saw that the driver of the car was staring down at her, his face pale with shock. 'I'm fine, thank you,' she said. 'Please, don't worry. It wasn't your fault.'

The child's mother looked on, horrified. 'You saved her life,' she said. 'I can't thank you enough for what you did. Are you sure that you're all right?'

Laura nodded. 'I'm sure. You go and keep your appointment. I'll be fine.' She struggled to get to her feet. Her arm was sore, but she didn't think it was too bad, and then all the effort became unnecessary because Nick appeared by her side and gave her a helping hand.

'I'll take care of her,' he said to the people standing by, and slowly they drifted away. Turning back to Laura, he said with a frown, 'Will you be able to walk, or shall I carry you?'

'I can walk,' Laura said quickly. 'Really, it's nothing, just a graze. Luckily he was driving at a reasonable speed, or it might have been worse.'

'I saw what happened,' he said. 'I was coming from the car park, but even from that distance I saw that it was some collision. I was sure that you must be badly hurt. I raced over here, almost expecting to find you unconscious.'

'Obviously I'm made of stronger stuff.'

He smiled. 'I'm glad of that. We'll check you over, just to make sure.'

'There's no need. My shift starts in a little while. I need to get ready for that.'

Nick shook his head. 'You're not going to do any-thing, until I've made sure that you're not hurt.'

He was still arguing with Laura when they entered A and E, and he thrust her firmly but gently into a cubicle. 'Sit down, be quiet and let me see what the damage is.'

'I told you, I'm perfectly all right, and I don't need you of all people checking me over.'

'There is no one else, and I don't have a minor injuries unit that I can send you to. All the staff here are busy treating patients, and if you don't let me get on with it, there are going to be a lot of people filling up the waiting room who won't be attended to this afternoon. Do I make myself clear?'

He was making himself very clear. He wasn't taking no for an answer, and she resigned herself to the fact that he was going to deal with her injuries, whether she liked it or not.

'Now, let's see. The car caught you on your shoulder, didn't it? Are you hurt anywhere else?'

'Nowhere.' She wasn't going to tell him, even if she was.

He looked at her doubtfully, but he didn't argue. 'OK, let's take your arm through a range of movement so that we can see what it is that we're dealing with.'

His hands were broad and masculine, his fingers long and inherently strong, but she marvelled at his gentle touch. He was infinitely careful as he examined her, but even so she winced a little as he tested her ability to use her shoulder.

'I don't think there's any lasting damage there,' he murmured, 'but you've certainly wrenched the liga-ments. You'll have to be cautious with it for a while.'

His glance shifted to her skinny ribbed top, a scoop-necked affair with short sleeves and buttons down the front. 'Perhaps you'd better undo a few buttons so that I can look at the graze.'

'There's really no need. You said that there's no lasting damage.'

His mouth twisted. 'You're bleeding,' he pointed out. 'So much that it has stained your sleeve. I suggest that you stop giving me a hard time and let me get on with examining you.'

A flush of heat ran along her cheekbones, but she figured that the sooner she did as he asked, the sooner this would all be over with.

She undid a couple of buttons and pulled at the shoulder of the garment, thankful that it was made of a stretchy material.

He looked closely at her creamy skin, marred by a gash that was red and angry-looking. 'That's a nasty wound,' he remarked evenly. 'I'll clean it up for you.'

He was thorough, making sure that no grit from the road had entered the wound.

'It doesn't look too bad,' he said. 'I don't think you'll need a stitch, but I'll put a couple of butterfly plasters on it to hold the edges of the cut together. You'll need to keep an eye on it to see that it heals properly.'

'I will.'

He drew the sleeve of her top down a little more so that he could fix the plasters in place, and she coloured again as the action exposed the lacy edge of her bra and the smooth, velvet slope of her breast.

He said lightly, 'I think that should do the trick.' There was a faint huskiness to his voice, and she felt all of a sudden as though the room was sparking with tension.

She sent him a quick, hooded glance, but he appeared to be concentrating on his handiwork. Perhaps she was imagining things. After all, it had been a crazy kind of day so far and her emotions were all over the place.

'So…did you go ahead with trying to find your mother?' He drew her sleeve up over her shoulder and began to clear away the equipment he had used.

She wondered if he could feel her nervousness and was trying to divert her, but she went along with it all the same.

'Yes, I did,' she said quietly, 'but I didn't get very far. I had her name and address, but the place doesn't exist any more. I'm not sure what my next move should be.'

He considered that for a moment or two. 'What name did you have?'

'Somerville. That's the name I had before I was adopted.'

'Hmm. You told me that you thought your father had died in an accident. A lot of time has gone by since then, and it could be that your mother married again.'

She stared at him. 'That hadn't occurred to me. Of course, you could be right.'

'If I am, you'll probably need to look at the register of marriages. It shouldn't be too difficult to find out if she remarried, although you might need to check other counties in case she moved away from the area.'

Nick reached out and laid a hand lightly on her un-injured arm. 'You know that I'm here to help you if you want me to? You only have to say the word.'

'Yes, I know… I'll…I'll remember that.' He held her gaze steadily, but she looked away.

He was being thoughtful and considerate, and as much as she was finding herself drawn towards him, as much as she might want to put her faith in him, how could she? How could she ask him for help, and join forces with him, when he was the one who could ultimately be responsible for putting her father out of a job?

She had to resist this growing feeling of intimacy that was binding her to Nick.

She owed her loyalty to her father, didn't she?

CHAPTER SEVEN

NO MATTER how uncertain her feelings were about Nick, Laura knew that she wouldn't be able to avoid him. She had to go on working with him on an almost daily basis, and in those circumstances all she could do was to try and keep up a calm and professional relationship with him.

'How is the woman from the car accident the other day?' Laura asked him a few days later. 'Have you had any follow-up information on her?'

'The MRI scan showed some bruising and swelling around the spinal cord,' he said, 'but I think she might make a full recovery in time. She began to feel some tingling in her legs on the day after she was admitted.'

'That's a relief.'

'It is, though her injured vertebrae mean that she'll have to wear a fixed neck and head brace for some time.'

'That's a whole lot better than ending up paralysed,' Laura commented.

'Very true.' He reached for a patient's chart, and then looked at her closely. 'I heard that Connor was discharged from hospital yesterday. You must be very pleased about that.'

'I am. It's brilliant. He's like a little ray of sunshine.' She laughed, thinking about him. 'Apparently he's hardly stayed still since he got back home. Matthew thinks he's trying to make up for lost time by getting up to as much mischief as possible. He and Catherine are so pleased to have him back that they can't bring themselves to tell him off for anything.'

'That's understandable.' He smiled. 'And how's your shoulder? Does it feel any easier?'

'It's as good as new, thanks.' She lowered her head momentarily, not wanting him to see the heat that filled her cheeks. The memory of his gentle touch was something that she was still struggling with.

'Good. I'm glad to hear it. That was a tremendously brave thing that you did, rescuing the little girl. I was afraid that you might have been hurt badly.'

'It was nothing.' She looked up at him and said, 'I still feel that you shouldn't have had to attend to me. This is an A and E department and there are far more important calls on your time.'

His blue-grey eyes moved over her, leaving a trail of heat in their wake. 'Maybe, but there was no way I was going to stand by and see you hurt.'

A faint line etched its way into his brow. 'I've already talked to your father about the possibility of setting up a minor injuries unit. He had already broached the idea with management, and they are looking at ways to organise it. It will take some of the heat off the A and E department if we can rely on simply having to treat the people who are most ill.'

She frowned. 'Have you thought about how all this is going to be funded?'

'Of course I have. Management has resources available, and it's just a question of how the funds are allocated.'

'Don't you think they might call for cuts to be made elsewhere?'

'That's always a possibility, but they have several options to choose from. What they have to consider is whether the changes they put in place will help to make things more efficient. There's a lot of talk these days about seeing as many patients as possible and cutting down on waiting times. What we want to put in place will help with all of those things.'

She was silent, wondering whether her father's position here would be safe, and she became conscious of Nick studying her features attentively.

'Perhaps you shouldn't worry so much about what's going on,' he suggested. 'You have enough on your mind as it is. How is the search for your mother going? Have you made any progress?'

She accepted his change of subject with a fairly easy grace. It was difficult for her to reconcile the problems that arose because of the differing responsibilities that Nick and her father carried, and perhaps it was a struggle best avoided where possible.

'I'm not sure,' she murmured. 'I've checked a number of registers, but there was no match for a woman with her birth date getting married in this county. I'm working my way through the neighbouring counties at the moment.'

She paused, feeling despondent for a moment, but then picked herself up. 'I've waited this long. I dare say I can put up with waiting for a bit longer, and at least I've been able to hand over some of the work to a woman from the records office. She was really helpful, and she said she would look through the microfilm and let me know if she came up with anything.'

Nick might have answered, but Sarah signalled that another emergency was coming in, and the team readied themselves for action. Things were chaotic for some time after that, and later, when she had hoped that the hectic pace might have begun to die down, Laura had to assess another patient who gave her cause to worry.

She called Nick over and asked his advice. 'Mrs Hanley was brought in after suffering from a severe bout of gastroenteritis, which we think may have started after she ate some shellfish. I'm not happy with her condition.'

'I'll come and have a look at her,' he said, and Laura felt an immediate rush of relief. She knew that she could rely on Nick. He was always calm and efficient and he would know what needed to be done.

'Have you sent samples to the lab for analysis?' he asked as he walked with her to the cubicle where Mrs Hanley lay, looking desperately ill.

'Yes, of course, but I'm still waiting to hear from them. In the meantime, I'm giving her broad-spectrum antibiotics. She's on oxygen and an infusion of glucose and saline, but her blood pressure is falling. Her breathing and her heart rate have increased. I'm afraid that this is a battle I'm not winning. She seems to be going downhill very rapidly.'

Nick carefully examined Mrs Hanley, and inspected her charts. 'She's suffering from septicaemia,' he said. 'It can turn very quickly to septic shock, so we need to get the right antibiotics into her as soon as possible. You'd better see if you can get her transferred to Intensive Care. While you're waiting for a bed for her, put her on vasoactive drugs, along with sympathomimetics, to maintain the blood pressure…and get on to the lab again. We need to know what organism we're dealing with.'

Laura hurried to put his advice into action. There was no time to lose, but everything depended on getting the right drug to treat the infection.

By the end of the afternoon her patient had been transferred to Intensive Care, and Laura took advantage of a lull in activity to go and take a break outside. She walked along a path that led to a landscaped area to one side of the hospital, stretching her aching limbs and enjoying the warm sunshine. It was a beautiful summer's day, and the sky was a clear, vivid blue. In the distance she could see the mountains, a mix of hazy blues and greens that was agreeable on the eyes.

It was peaceful out there, and she sought out her favourite place, a secluded little arbour where she could sit on a bench and listen to the birdsong. It was so different to the sometimes frantic atmosphere in A and E.

She wasn't left alone for very long. Nick appeared, looking cool and fresh. In A and E he had been wearing an immaculate dark grey suit, which gave him a commanding presence, but now he had abandoned the jacket and his shirt was a pleasing contrast, looking crisp and clean, with pale self-coloured stripes.

'I thought I might find you here,' he said. 'There was a phone call for you. Sarah took a message.' He handed her a slip of paper. 'I think this might be what you've been looking for.'

Laura opened out the paper that he had given her and studied it. 'Emma Sherwin', she read. 'Formerly Somerville.' Then there followed a date of marriage and an address.

She lifted her gaze to Nick, her eyes brilliant with joy. 'I've found her,' she exclaimed. 'I've found my mother.'

'That's wonderful news,' Nick said.

'I never imagined it would happen so soon. Isn't it fantastic?' She moved towards him, her body fizzing with excitement. 'She's living near Wrexham, just a couple of hours' drive away. I can go and see her. I'll be able to talk to her.' Her mouth curved in a smile. 'I hardly dared dream that this would happen. Oh, Nick, I'm so happy.'

'I'm happy for you.' He smiled with her, and reached out to give her a hug. She went willingly into his arms, her face tilted up to him, a delightful tide of exhilaration washing through her veins, and when he lowered his head and tenderly, almost hesitantly brushed her lips with his own, it seemed the most natural thing in the world.

His kiss was gentle, warm and inviting, and the surge of pleasure it stirred in her was totally unexpected. It thrilled her to the core. Her head was swimming, and she didn't know quite what was making her dizzy, whether it was the news she had just received or the sweet, tantalising caress of his mouth exploring hers. It didn't seem to matter right then. Nothing mattered. There was only this feeling that everything in the world was joyous and complete.

It was only when the sound of approaching footsteps infiltrated the mist that had invaded her mind that she began to realise what was happening. Nick was kissing her, and that wasn't how things were supposed to be.

She dragged her mouth from his and tried to draw back from him, looking up at him with troubled eyes, confusion clouding her mind. He hesitated, and then reluctantly let her go.

'Nick, I...'

He shook his head as though to clear it. 'I'm sorry. I don't know how that happened... I don't know what I was thinking. You looked so happy, so elated. It was instinct, I think. I felt that I needed to share it with you, and things got out of hand.'

She didn't know what to say to him. The truth was,

she had never reacted in such a way to a kiss before this. Her senses had soared, rising chaotically along with the thunder of her pulse. She was left feeling distracted, overwhelmed, her emotions in total disarray.

'We'll try to forget that it happened, shall we?' she mumbled.

He nodded slowly. 'If that's what you want.'

'I think it might be for the best.' She stood up. 'I'd better get back to work.' She began to walk back along the path and he followed her.

'You said that your mother lives near Wrexham. I have to go over there at the weekend. My brother has a laptop computer that he's getting rid of, and I said that I would go and collect it from him. I could take you over there if you like. I could drop you off at your mother's house and then come and collect you later to bring you back home again.'

'I'm not sure,' Laura said. After what had just happened, perhaps she ought to try to put some distance between them. 'It may not turn out as I expect. She might not be there, or she might not want to see me. Things could go wrong.'

'I won't just abandon you there,' he said with a laugh. 'You can trust me to look after you properly.' He regarded her steadily. 'I mean it. You can trust me.'

She returned his gaze awkwardly. 'I know... I know. I need time to think.'

'Of course you do. This has all come as a bit of a shock, hasn't it? Anyway, whatever you decide to do with such a long journey ahead of you, it will probably work out better if you give your mother a call and warn her that you're coming.'

By now they had reached the doors of the hospital,

and he laid a hand lightly in the small of her back as he guided her into the building.

'Take your time to think things through,' he said, 'but remember, there is no point in both of us driving all that way when it would be more practical for us to share the journey.'

She nodded. She couldn't find any words to answer him just then, because her senses were clamouring once more, thrown into hectic disorder by the gentle touch of his hand resting warmly on her spine.

Back in A and E, she checked up on the patient she had sent to Intensive Care. The laboratory had discovered which organism was causing the woman's illness, and now it was possible that a specific treatment could be found. She hoped that they were not too late for it to do some good.

When the weekend arrived, she agreed to let Nick take her to find her mother. As he had said, it was impractical for them both to make the same journey separately.

'I think I should talk to her on my own,' she said. 'It will probably be overwhelming enough for her to have me turn up out of the blue like this, and she might not be happy to see another stranger alongside me.'

'I think you could be right about that,' Nick answered, 'but this is bound to be a traumatic time for you, too, and you ought to have someone with you this first time.'

Deep down, she agreed with him on that score. She had still not told her father what she was doing, and nobody but Nick knew about this visit.

She was nervous, beset by doubts. Was she doing the right thing? How would her adoptive mother have felt about what she was doing now? She felt compelled to go on with this now that she had started, she needed to resolve this situation once and for all, but it didn't mean that she loved her any the less. Her adoptive mother had loved her and cared for her, and nothing could ever take the place of that.

Nick called for her around mid-morning on Saturday when her father was out, and as she opened her front door to him she realised how glad she was to see him. She wanted him to be with her. He was dressed in casual chinos and a light-coloured shirt, and he looked incredibly attractive.

'Did you talk to your mother on the phone?' he asked, but she shook her head.

'She wasn't there, but I spoke to her husband. He was shocked to hear from me, I think, but he said that he would pass the message on and get back to me.'

'And he arranged for you to go over there today?'

'Yes, he rang back a few hours later, giving me directions as to how to find them.'

'Let's get started, then.'

They found the house fairly quickly. It was in a tree-lined avenue, a quiet, pretty area, not too far from the sea.

'I'll wait here in the car, as we arranged,' Nick said, when she stepped out onto the pavement and prepared to go and ring the doorbell. 'I know this is something very personal to you and I don't want to intrude. Just give me a nod if everything seems all right, and I'll leave you and go over to my brother's house. Give me a call on my mobile when you're ready for me to pick you up again.'

'I will. Thanks.' She gave him a brief smile and went up to the house.

A man answered the door. He was in his mid-fifties, she guessed, with strong brown hair that was showing streaks of grey. He had a kind, well-worn face, and she took to him almost immediately.

'Come in, Laura,' Roger Sherwin said. 'I expect you'd like a cup of tea after your long journey. Let's go through to the kitchen, shall we, and I'll put the kettle on?'

'Thank you.' She turned and nodded to Nick, and after a moment he started up the engine and drove away.

'Have you lived here long?' Laura asked after a few minutes, when she was sipping tea in the sun-filled conservatory, which backed on to the kitchen.

'About fifteen years,' Roger told her. 'Your mother fell in love with the house as soon as she saw it.'

Laura smiled in appreciation. 'I can see why.' The conservatory looked out onto a paved patio and a garden that was in full bloom. On the patio there was a white-painted wooden wheelbarrow, which had been filled with bright petunias and trailing lobelia, and in a corner of the garden there was a raised area that had been paved and decorated with tubs that were overflowing with blossom. 'Who does the gardening?' she asked.

'Your mother. She was always very keen to see it looking good.'

'Is she still not here?' Laura was suddenly besieged by doubt. 'Did she change her mind about wanting to see me?'

Roger shook his head. 'She wants to see you more than anything. She left her contact address all those years ago so that you could get in touch if you wanted to. Then, when we married, we had to move away because of my work. I don't know why you weren't given her new name and address. We did notify the agency, but when you told me of the difficulties you had in finding us, I phoned to ask them what had happened. They were apologetic and said that possibly it was down to human error and the details weren't transferred to your file. It was a slip-up that could have caused tremendous problems.'

'Did she remember me? I mean, did her memory come back? I wasn't sure whether she would have lost those years for ever.'

'It came back gradually, in bits and pieces, over the years that she was with me. I do know that she has been longing to see you for as far back as I can remember. She would have sent cards and presents, but the agency was very much against that. They said you had been confused by what had happened when you were ill, that you had made up an imaginary friend, almost like a comfort blanket to get you through the situation, and that any contact would have made you even more troubled.'

Laura glanced quickly at him. 'An imaginary friend?'

He gave her a brief smile. 'They said that she seemed very real to you at the time.'

Laura frowned. Was that what she had been remembering lately, a child she had conjured up to help her through a troubled time?

'I don't remember any of that,' she said quietly. She glanced around. 'But where is my mother? She still isn't here.' She was becoming anxious all at once. 'Is something wrong?'

'I'm afraid so.' Roger looked unhappy and for a moment she had the impression that he was struggling to compose himself.

'What is it? You must tell me, please.'

'She's ill, I'm afraid. Seriously ill. And we don't know what the outcome will be. We were hoping that it was something she could fight, but instead it's taken hold of her and it's dragging her down. She's in hospital. The doctors don't know if she will recover.'

Laura felt the blood drain from her face. 'What's wrong with her?'

'She has leukaemia. She started to become ill some months ago, and they've tried everything possible. I'm so sorry to have to tell you this. I thought it better that I told you face to face rather than deliver a message like that over the phone.'

Laura felt numb inside. She didn't know what to say or do, but simply stared into space for a while, trying to take it in.

After a few minutes she pulled herself together and talked to Roger about his life with her mother, and what had happened in the intervening years since she had left her daughter behind.

'I'd still like to see her. Did you tell her that I came looking for her?' she asked.

He nodded and then gave her a bleak smile. 'It made her very happy to know that you wanted to meet her.'

Some time later Laura rang Nick, and he arrived within a few minutes. Laura said goodbye to Roger and walked out to the car, feeling empty and lost, not knowing what to do.

Nick looked at her in concern as she slid into the passenger seat. 'Did it go badly? Tell me what happened.'

She told him, and he sat for a moment in silence, staring out of the windscreen at the road ahead. Then he started the engine and drove away from the house.

'Where are we going?' Laura asked after a while, rousing herself to take note of their surroundings.

'To the hospital, so that you can see your mother. Isn't that where you want to go?'

'Yes. I do…but I can't think straight. I'm still trying to take it all in. It's been really hard to get so far, and then find that she's desperately ill. I'm not sure that I know how to cope with everything.'

'Just remember that you're not alone in this,' he reminded her softly. 'I know it feels bad, but I'm here with you, and together we can face up to it.'

She felt comforted by his words. He was her strength right now, her defence against the world and everything bad that it had to throw at her. She could lean on him, just for a little while, and he would help her absorb the hurt.

Her mother was asleep when they walked quietly into her room. Her hair was tousled, wispy after the treatment she had undergone, but Laura could see that her curls were a soft honey gold.

'Be careful not to disturb her,' the nurse warned. 'She needs all the rest she can get.'

'I will.'

Laura sat by her mother's bedside and watched her, and felt an outpouring of love for this woman who had been through so much. Her eyes filled with tears and she dashed them away, angry with herself for giving in to them.

Nick put his arm around her and folded her to him, and she laid her head against his chest, taking strength from its solid warmth and the steady beat of his heart.

After a few minutes her mother stirred from her sleep and slowly opened her eyes. 'Sophie?' she said softly.

Laura frowned fleetingly, then leaned forward and gently stroked her hand. Her mother was very frail and it wasn't surprising that she was confused.

She hesitated. What should she call her? Mother? Mum? It seemed so strange to use either of those when they had only just met and were virtual strangers. 'Emma…' she said at last, her voice husky, 'I'm Laura. I'm your daughter. I had to find you, I had to come and see you.'

'Laura? My little girl?' Her mother's smile was beautiful and, ill as she was, it lit up her face. 'You were so little when I last saw you…you looked at me with such big eyes.' She was silent for a while, remembering, and then she closed her eyes as though the effort had worn her out.

Laura wondered if she had drifted into sleep, but then her mother said softly, 'This is the happiest day of my life. I've waited for this day for so long. I didn't think it would ever happen.'

'I'm here now,' Laura said softly. 'I'm so glad that I've found you.'

The nurse came and put her head round the door just a short time later and told them that they must leave. Laura watched her mother drift back into sleep and then quietly followed the nurse out of the room.

'Is there anything that can be done for her?' she asked softly.

'Her only hope is a bone-marrow transplant,' the nurse said, 'but up to now that hasn't been possible. We haven't been able to find a suitable match.'

'Perhaps I'll be able to help,' Laura said quickly. 'Take a blood sample from me, here and now, and we'll see whether I can be a donor.'

'All right.'

The procedure took a matter of minutes, and when she had finished the nurse wrote out the forms and said, 'I'll send this off to the lab, and we'll contact you as soon as we have any news.'

'Thank you.'

'Come on,' Nick said, when they were out in the corridor once more, 'there's nothing more you can do today. I'll take you home.'

'I suppose you're right.' She swallowed hard, making an effort to bring her emotions under control. 'We'd better go. I need to get back and tell my father what I've been doing.'

Nick lifted a dark brow. 'You're going to tell him that you've found your mother? That's a change of heart, isn't it? I thought you were hesitant about doing that in case it upset him.'

'He's had a lot on his mind lately, and I didn't want to burden him with it, but it's done now, and I would sooner he heard the news from me than from anyone else.'

'I think you're doing the right thing.'

She nodded. 'Thank you for being with me today. I don't know how I would have got through it without you.'

'I told you that I would be here for you,' he said quietly, 'and I meant it.'

Nick held her close and she closed her eyes and for a few moments she gave in to the wonderful feeling of being protected and secure.

Then she said softly, 'It felt so strange, meeting her after all this time…almost unreal, and then when she called me Sophie I was anxious for a while.'

'Do you think there is someone called Sophie who might be related to you in some way?'

'I don't know.' She frowned. 'I don't think so, but Roger told me that I made up an imaginary friend as a child. I suppose it's possible that I might have called her Sophie. The name certainly rings a bell, and perhaps that was why the name came into my mother's mind. I don't remember.' She looked up at him. 'That could explain why I've been having all these odd feelings just lately. I always thought something was missing from my child-hood, but it was such a mixed-up time and I must have made her up to help me through it.'

'A lot of children do that, especially when they're troubled. Maybe it makes things easier for them for a while.' He smiled down at her. 'Let's get you home.'

'All right.' He was still holding her close, but now she gently extricated herself from his arms and walked with him to his car.

The short walk helped to clear her head. She felt closer to Nick than she had ever done before, but some instinct of self-preservation told her that giving in to her feelings would only serve to cause her more grief in the end.

Nick wasn't going to be her salvation. He was offering her comfort because it was the human thing to do, and even though this heightened awareness sparked between them, it would do her no good in the end. He was still the one who could bring about her father's downfall, and how could she square her feelings with that? Her father wouldn't thank her for allying herself with him.

CHAPTER EIGHT

'Look at me, Aunty Lor,' Connor said. 'I'm a bird.' He jumped off the low wall that bordered the garden at the front of the house and then began to flap his arms like wings as he raced around on the lawn.

'You're a very busy bird,' Laura said, smiling at him and hoping that his mother had told him only to jump off low-level objects.

'I wish I had that much energy this early in the day,' her father said, watching his grandson with amusement.

'Me, too.' Laura watched as Catherine came and gathered Connor's things together, readying her son for the journey home.

'I hope he calms down before this afternoon,' Catherine murmured. 'I don't think it will go down too well if he starts to race around the hospital waiting room like this. We've got an appointment there, but I'm almost tempted to say that he doesn't need a check-up. Anyone can tell just by looking at him that he's fully back to normal.' She made a wry face. 'Best to be on the safe side though.'

She watched Connor make a beeline for the ornamental cherry tree that draped its branches low over one corner of the garden. 'Connor, don't you dare pull those branches.'

'I'll go and see to him,' Laura's father said.

Glancing at Laura, Catherine said lightly, 'Your consultant...Nick Hilliard, isn't it? He said that he would show us round the new paediatric wing while we are there this afternoon. It's not quite ready yet, but he thought Connor might like to look around.' She laughed. 'If you ask me, he's keen on getting a child's point of view so he knows if everything's looking as it should.'

'That sounds like something that Nick would do,' Laura agreed drily.

'He's really dishy, isn't he?' Catherine murmured. 'You are lucky to be working with someone like him.'

Laura made a wry face. She was all too conscious of Nick's good looks.

Catherine looked around and tracked her son's movements as he headed up the path. 'Come on, Connor, let's get you into the car.'

Laura and her father waved goodbye as she drove away a short time later.

'I shall have to make a move soon, too,' her father said, as they walked back into the house. 'There's a stack of work I need to go through before my meeting.'

Laura gave him a quick glance. He wasn't showing any outward signs of unease, but she knew that he was apprehensive about this morning's talks with his superiors.

'Perhaps it will just be a general discussion,' she said, 'and not anything to do with job cuts after all.'

He didn't look as though he was convinced of that. 'Possibly. The letter just says that they want to talk about the shape of future plans and how they might impinge on staff.'

'But you think that your job might be at risk, don't you?' Laura walked into the kitchen and began to clear coffee-cups from the table. 'Have they told you that?'

'There have been hints so far, but nothing more. The meeting might help to clarify things. I'll talk to you about it this evening—which reminds me, I'll be out until fairly late tonight. I'm having supper with a friend.'

He watched her load the dishwasher. 'You're on the late shift again today, aren't you? Are you going to see your mother this morning?'

'Yes. If I leave in a minute or so, I should have time to get there and back before my shift starts.'

She sent him a cautious glance. 'I sprang it on you a bit, didn't I, the other night, telling you that I'd started to look for her? I hadn't really expected to find her so soon. Did you mind that I went ahead without telling you first? I was worried about doing it, and I know you said that it was all right, but it must have come as a shock.'

He shook his head. 'No, love, I didn't mind. I was fairly sure that you would want to look for her one day. It was always going to be there, niggling away at the back of your mind, so I can't say that it was totally unexpected. I know how important it must have been for you to find her. I just didn't want you to get hurt, that's all. I was afraid that she might have made a new life for herself and that she wouldn't want to know you.'

'I think she was pleased to see me. Even though she's desperately ill, she looked happy.'

'I'm glad about that.' He searched her face. 'But how do you feel about finding her now that you've had time to take it all in?'

Laura considered his question thoughtfully. 'I'm not sure. Unsettled, I think. And guilty, because I wish Mum had been alive so that I could talk it over with her. I want her blessing—more than anything, I want to know that she wouldn't have minded. She was the best mother in the world.'

He smiled. 'She knew that you loved her. When you

were little, she worried that you might pine for your real mother. She was very protective of you. You had been through so much and you were vulnerable, and she didn't want you to suffer any more hurt. But she was secure enough in your relationship with her as you grew older. We even talked about the time when you might want to find your natural mother, and I think she was prepared for that. She knew that she would never lose you.'

'If she were here, I would be able to tell her that she needn't worry. I love you both so very much. You know that, don't you?'

'I do. And so did your mother. I know that she would want you to be happy and she would have encouraged you to do what you thought was right. I'm only concerned that this works out for you the way you want it to.'

He looked at her carefully. 'You said that you feel unsettled. Do you want to talk about it?'

'I don't know why I feel that way. I suppose I had hoped that I would feel complete once I found her, as though all the things that have been troubling me over the years would miraculously vanish, but it hasn't happened. Instead, I feel edgy and uptight, and as though everything's askew.'

'That's probably because your mother is ill. You weren't expecting that, and it must have come as a shock.'

'Perhaps. I might feel differently once I have the results of the blood test. I'm desperate to know whether or not I can be a bone-marrow donor, but until then it's as though I can't move forward. Everything's in limbo, so to speak.'

'You're doing everything that you can. And on the

positive side, it must have given your mother a lift just to know that you'd found her and that you get on well together.'

'I hope so.'

By the time Laura's shift started later that day, Connor was already doing the tour of the new paediatric emergency unit, and she went along to see how he was doing.

Nick was showing him the room where children would wait to be assessed by a triage nurse before going for treatment. 'Go and see what there is for you to play with, if you like,' he told Connor. 'There's a home corner, and a puzzle table… Or you might want to have a go with some of the construction toys.'

Connor didn't need telling twice. He shot across the room and delved into a bright box that was overflowing with all kinds of goodies.

With a whoop of joy he pulled out two action figures. 'They've got firemen,' he shouted. 'I like these… And there's a fire engine…' He started to make a sound like a siren, and then extended the ladder on the fire engine and placed the fireman on top.

'I think we can confidently say that this place has his approval,' Catherine said.

Laura grinned. 'How did his check-up go?'

'Just as I expected. He's fine.' She watched as Connor rummaged in the box. 'I'd better go and keep an eye on him.'

Nick leaned back against a tall cupboard, his long legs stretched out, his thumbs hooked casually in his trouser pockets. He looked devastatingly attractive, powerfully masculine, and Laura's pulse began to race just from looking at him.

'And what do you think of our new unit?' he asked her.

Laura was glad of the distraction. Just lately she had become far too conscious that Nick was thoroughly, bone-meltingly male.

She looked around at the cheerful murals and then up at the ceiling, which had been decorated to look like a summer sky with birds soaring on high. 'It's very impressive,' she said. 'I think this will certainly help to take children's minds off their injuries, provided they aren't too bad. Does the rest of the department live up to this standard?'

'I believe it does. We're still bringing in the equipment, but it's completely up to date, and alongside that we've several resuscitation cubicles and a dozen more for general paediatric treatment.'

'You must be very proud of what you've achieved in such a short time.'

'I'm more satisfied with the fact that children will be seen quickly and that hopefully they will be less traumatised when they need medical attention,' he said. 'That's what this has all been about from the first.'

'I understand that,' she murmured. She looked around and lapsed into silence, preoccupied.

'Have you been see your mother again?' he asked, and she nodded. 'How is she?'

'Very ill. She was confused again, and she still seems to be muddling me up with someone called Sophie. I suppose that's only to be expected after all this time. It can't be easy for her to keep a grasp on the situation when she's fighting for her life.'

'But she does know that you're her daughter?'

'Yes, I'm sure she knows that.'

She stayed for a few more minutes, looking around the unit with Nick, and then said, 'I must go and start work. You're on duty today as well, aren't you?'

He nodded. 'Yes. I'll be along in half an hour.'

Laura said goodbye to Catherine and Connor and went to A and E next door. She was busy for the next few hours with road accident victims and a variety of domestic injuries.

A teenage girl came in with a nosebleed, and Laura sat her down in a chair and instructed her to keep her head tilted slightly forward, and showed her how to pinch her nose near to the end.

'It's been bleeding like this for two hours now,' her mother said. 'I didn't know what to do to stop it.'

'They're usually nothing much to worry about,' Laura told her. She gave her patient some tissues and a dish to hold. 'Just in case there are any drips,' she said. 'Try to breathe through your mouth.'

Some twenty minutes later, the girl's nose was still bleeding. 'What we'll do is to pack your nose with gauze,' Laura said. 'The gauze is soaked in something that will help to stop the bleeding, and the pressure from the gauze against the blood vessels will help as well.'

'Now, there's a case that would have been well served by a minor injuries unit,' Nick said, as he watched Laura discharge her patient an hour later.

'I dare say. I expect you'll have that up and running before too much longer.'

She went off to tend to a child who had scalded himself, advising his mother about keeping the dressing in place, and Nick was there by her side once again as she sent her a small patient home with instructions for aftercare to be carried out by the family's GP practice.

'It's never easy, is it, dealing with a child who has that kind of injury?' Nick murmured.

'No, it isn't. I don't know how I would cope if I had

children of my own,' Laura answered. 'I don't think I could bear to see them in pain.'

Sarah hurried towards them just then. 'There's a phone call for you, Laura. It's the hospital where your mother is a patient.'

Laura rushed away to take the call. She didn't think that anything would have happened to her mother since she had spoken to her that morning. This had to be about the blood test.

The nurse who broke news did her best to soften the blow, but it hit Laura hard all the same. She wasn't going to be able to be a donor.

'I'm so sorry,' the nurse said. 'I know this isn't the news you wanted to hear.'

Laura replaced the receiver and stumbled outside, feeling leaden. She needed to get some air. It was a warm evening, but she still shivered. Her legs were weak and she sat down shakily on a bench that looked out onto a small quadrangle.

'What did they say? Is your mother all right?' Nick came and sat next to her.

Laura shook her head. 'I can't be a donor. I'm not a suitable match.' She turned to him, her features anguished. 'How can this be happening?' she said. 'I've only just found her. How can I lose her now before I've even had a chance to get to know her properly?'

Nick put his arm around her and held her close. Tears trickled down her cheeks and this time she didn't try to hide them. He drew her to him, and she nestled against his broad chest, resting her head in the crook of his shoulder, taking refuge in his nearness. He stroked her hair as she cried, his fingers tangling in the silk of her curls.

Gradually her tears subsided, and she rubbed at her face with a hanky that he provided.

'She's still relatively young,' she said, a tremor in her voice. 'Sometimes life can be wretched.'

'And in our job we're in a position to see that more than most people,' Nick agreed.

Laura straightened up. 'I suppose I ought to go and show my face in A and E,' she said. 'They'll be wondering what's happened to me.'

'You don't need to worry about that. Let me take you home. We're both due to go off duty about now, anyway.'

The way she was trembling, Laura didn't think she would be able to drive herself back home, but she said, 'How can you do that? We came to work in separate cars.'

'It doesn't matter. I'll drive yours, and I'll get a taxi back to mine. Given the state you're in, I don't want you to drive yourself.'

'I'll be all right in a while. I just need to get myself together.'

He shook his head. 'I'm not listening to any arguments. I've already made up my mind. I'm taking you home.'

The house was empty when they arrived there some thirty minutes later. 'I think my father has gone to dinner with a friend,' she said. 'He mentioned something about it this morning.' She pushed open the front door. 'Will you come in for a coffee? You can ring for a taxi from here in a while. I've got the number somewhere.'

'Thanks. I'd like that.'

She went into the kitchen and started to spoon coffee into the percolator. 'It shouldn't take too long to brew.

Can I get you anything else while we wait? A sandwich, or something?'

He shook his head. 'I grabbed something to eat at the hospital.' He hesitated, and then said, 'I've been thinking about what you said the other day—about your mother mistakenly calling you Sophie. It started off a train of thought in my head, and there's something I'd like to check up on. I wonder…do you have your birth certificate to hand? I know it's a strange request but would you mind if I take a look at it?'

The request startled her, but she said, 'I don't mind. I think it's in the bureau. I'll go fetch it for you.' She started to go towards the living room, then added lightly, 'There's nothing interesting about it. It seems quite straightforward to me.'

While they waited for the coffee to percolate, Nick studied the certificate. Laura watched him, and then said quietly, 'See? I told you there was nothing special about it. It just shows my mother's name, and where I was born, and it gives my name. Absolutely nothing unusual, is there?'

'You're right. As you say, it's quite straightforward.' Even so, he looked thoughtful as he handed the certificate back to her.

She put it away in the bureau and then went back into the kitchen. 'I imagined that Sophie was just someone I conjured up. But do you think that she actually exists— that she was a friend, or a cousin, maybe?'

'I don't know. I have to think about it some more.' As they sipped their drinks a few minutes later, he asked, 'Have you talked to your mother's doctor about any alternative treatments?'

Laura nodded. 'They seem to have explored every av-

enue up to now. I don't think they have anything else
in mind.'

She reached up into a cupboard and took out a batch
of pasties that she had made earlier. She slid some onto
a plate and pushed it towards him. She didn't believe
that he wasn't hungry. A man who was that tall and that
energetic needed stoking up at regular intervals, she was
certain. Besides, it gave her something to do and helped
her to calm herself.

As she had expected, he casually stretched a hand out
for one and it disappeared in quick time. She arched a
brow. 'You'd better have another. I knew you couldn't
be telling the truth. I've seen you in the hospital restaurant. I know what an appetite you have...though to look
at you, no one would suspect it.' There wasn't an ounce
of fat on him. He was flat-stomached, lean and lithe,
constantly on the move.

He gave a crooked smile. 'You've caught me out. I
admit it. I must have been more hungry than I thought.'
He looked down at the pasty that was fast going the way
of the first. 'They do taste very good, though, so you
can hardly blame me, can you?'

Her mouth tilted at the corners. She was glad he had
come back to the house with her. She was beginning to
feel better, and it was all down to him. He drew her out
of herself somehow, and she had no idea how he managed it.

He swallowed his coffee. Looking at her over the rim
of his cup, he said, 'Shall we go over to the hospital
together tomorrow? Neither of us will be working, so
we could make a day of it. It could be upsetting for you,
seeing your mother again, and I'd like to go along with
you. I think you might find that you need some support,
and I want to be there for you.'

She was touched by his generosity. 'Thank you, that will be good. I'll give Roger a ring and tell him that we're going over there.' She hadn't been looking forward to going to the hospital alone. Being with her mother was an emotional experience, all the more fraught for the knowledge that these next few weeks might be all she would have with her.

He was watching her, and she tried not to notice how very distracting he was when he looked at her that way. His eyes were deeply blue-grey, sincere and compassionate, and he made her feel safe somehow in the knowledge that she wasn't on her own in this.

'You've been a great help to me,' she said softly. 'All this has been much more difficult than I ever imagined it would be. None of it is turning out the way I'd hoped.'

Nick put his cup down and came around the table towards her. 'I know that it's a testing time for you right now,' he said gently, 'but you should try to stay positive. There's always hope, and you should never give up.'

'I'll do my best,' she whispered.

'That's my girl.' He slid his hands around her waist and drew her to him. Then he lowered his head until his forehead came to rest lightly against hers, and she responded by putting her arms around him. They clung together, neither of them moving, but Laura was content to simply absorb the warmth and reassurance that he was offering.

It seemed completely natural to be standing there in that way. After a moment he bent his head and brushed his cheek against hers, in a soothing gesture, while he eased her against his body and began to run his hand in a smooth caress along her spine. When she turned her head slightly, his mouth was so close that it seemed perfectly right that their lips should meet.

He kissed her tenderly, his lips moving in warm exploration as though he would test out the softness of her mouth.

For a heady moment there was nothing in the world but this sweet temptation, this release from everything that was going wrong in her life. She clung to him, returning his kiss, savouring every wonderful moment.

She was so close to him that her soft curves melted against his strong body. She felt alive with sensation, her skin burning with need, feverish for his touch, and as if he understood, he ran his hands over her, cupping the softness of her breast, measuring its fullness with his hand.

A soft moan escaped her, and she almost swayed. Then he was moving back, away from her, yet still holding her, his hands around her arms keeping her steady, and she wondered what was happening, why he was all at once depriving her of succour.

'I think I just heard a car,' he said, his voice rough around the edges. 'Perhaps it's your father coming home.' He looked down at her, and he must have seen the flush of her cheeks, the cloudy bewilderment in her eyes.

As she gathered her senses and heard the key in the door, she began to realise how close she had come to behaving in a way that she would have come to regret. She wasn't ready for any of this. Her life was a mess, full of complications that she scarcely knew how to handle. How could she have been so reckless as to lose her senses this way?

She pulled herself together. 'You're right,' she said evenly. 'That does sound like my father coming home. I need to talk to him. He was worried this morning, there was a meeting...'

'I understand. I'll leave you to talk to him.' He walked towards the door, and he was already ringing for a taxi on his mobile. 'I'll call for you in the morning. Goodnight, Laura.'

'But…don't you want to wait for your taxi?'

'No, I'll get some air.'

'All right. Goodnight, then. I'll see you out.'

Her father was in the hall, and he and Nick exchanged a few brisk words before Nick left. Laura waited by the front door for a while until Nick's taxi appeared at the end of the avenue. She needed time to get herself together before she went in search of her father.

'How did the meeting go today?' There was an air of tension about him that made her concerned.

'They are still working out how they're going to implement all the cost-cutting. No decisions have been made yet, but they're definitely thinking about redundancies.' His mouth tightened. 'I think they'll look at people who are due to retire very soon first of all, and then at those who are just a few years away from retirement.'

'Like you, you mean?'

He nodded grimly. 'I have about another ten years before I should officially retire, and I was hoping that I would be able to keep going. I'd bargained without Nick, though. He comes in with all his ideas, and has no thought whatsoever for how they're going to affect other people. What does he care that there are still things I want to do? He thinks I'm old and past it, but I'm not ready to be put out to pasture just yet.' He grimaced. 'OK, the virus took a lot out of me, and it slowed me down for a while, but it doesn't mean that I'm ready for the scrapheap.'

Laura went and put her arms around him. 'Of course

you're not. We're going to fight this, you and me. We're not going to let it happen to you.'

Nick arrived early the next morning to take her to the hospital to see her mother. Laura felt awkward with him, remembering her father's hurt from the previous evening, and she was glad that he wasn't there to see her going off with Nick. All this put her in an impossible situation. How was she going to balance the two of them?

There had been no change in her mother's condition overnight, they learned, and the nurse told them that she had been sleeping on and off throughout the morning.

'Her husband came in to visit earlier, so she's very tired,' the nurse said. 'She loves these visits, but they tend to wear her out.'

She roused when Laura arrived, though, and said quietly, 'I'm so proud of you, Laura. Look at you... You're so beautiful, and a doctor, too. You've done well. I'm so glad that I've been able to see you before I go.'

'Don't say that, Emma. Please, don't say that. I need you to get well.'

Her mother smiled and closed her eyes, and Laura left after a while so that she could get the rest that she needed.

'I'd like to go and talk to Roger now,' Laura said as she and Nick went back to his car. 'This must be very hard for him.'

He nodded. 'We'll go there right away. Is he expecting you?'

'Yes, I rang him yesterday. I need to tell him about the result of the blood test, and he asked me if I would go and see him.'

'Good. I wanted to have a word with him myself.

There's something I want to clear up, something I don't quite understand.'

'What's that?'

'It may be nothing important,' he said with a negligent shrug. 'I'll see what he has to say first before I burden you with it.'

'Is this something to do with the birth certificate?'

'Yes, but there's no point discussing it until I've spoken to Roger.'

It was frustrating that he wouldn't say any more than that, and Laura resigned herself to waiting.

It had turned out to be another glorious summer's day, and Laura reflected on the irony of that as they sat out on Roger's patio. Her mother was terribly ill, but the sun was hot and brilliant, bathing them in its full glory. Roger put up a sun umbrella to shade them from its rays as they sipped iced drinks.

'I'm really upset because I can't be a donor for Emma,' she told him. 'I'm so sorry that I had to give you such bad news. I was praying that it would work out all right for all of us, but then the nurse from the hospital called with the result and it was shattering.'

'You did your best, and that's all that anyone can ask. Thank you for trying.' He looked at her with compassion. 'You look all in. Why don't you lean back and relax for a while?'

'I think I will.' It had been more of a strain than she had realised, seeing her mother looking so pale and ill. She leaned back in her chair and looked at the lovely garden. It was so unfair that her mother couldn't be sitting out here with them.

Nick got on well with Roger from the moment they met. The two men formed an instant rapport, and it was just as well, because while they were talking it gave her time to sit back and calm herself.

'Can I refill your glass?' Roger asked after a while, but she shook her head.

'I'm fine, thanks.'

'All right, then. Just help yourself if you want some more.' He turned back to Nick. 'What's this you were saying about the birth certificate? What makes you think there's something that we've overlooked?'

Laura sat up and started to pay attention.

'There are two things that I'm wondering about,' Nick explained. 'The first is that the certificate notes the actual time of day that Laura was born. That's quite unusual, I believe. It's mainly written down when there is more than one birth to be recorded—as with twins, for instance.'

Laura stared at Nick. That thought had never occurred to her. She glanced quickly at Roger, and saw that he was chewing his lip.

'Was there a twin?' she asked him. He was looking anxious and she wondered if something bad had happened in the past, along with everything else.

He didn't answer for a moment, and Nick added, 'The other thing that made me curious was that your wife has been mistaking Laura for someone else. Someone called Sophie. Do you know anything about that?'

Roger let out a slow breath, as though the subject was causing him some distress. 'I do,' he admitted, 'but I'm not sure that it's going to help us in any way.'

'Tell us,' Nick said. 'We've come this far, and I think Laura should know the whole story, don't you?'

Roger nodded. 'All right, then…but it's not a pleasant story.' He took a deep breath. 'Emma did give birth to twin girls…Laura and Sophie. They weren't identical, but they were born within minutes of each other. Laura is the older twin.'

He cleared his throat. 'You need to understand that Emma's relationship with her husband started to go wrong very soon after they married.'

He sent Laura a quick, apologetic look. 'I'm sorry to say this, Laura, but your father wasn't a kind man—not in the way he treated your mother at least. He wanted Emma to go and live in Switzerland, but Emma refused to go. She'd had enough of travelling, following him here, there and everywhere and living out of a suitcase. When you girls were born she started to put down roots here in Wales, and she didn't want to disrupt you when you were happy and settled. The marriage started to fall apart even more after that, and eventually he took up with someone else. Emma didn't know about the other woman to begin with, but when she found out she threatened him with divorce.'

He picked up his glass and took a long swallow. 'Your father became an angry and bitter man. He wanted to hurt your mother, and one day he simply picked up your sister from nursery school and took her out of the country. You were suffering with an ear infection at the time, and it was clear that you weren't well. You wouldn't have been allowed on the plane.'

'Are you saying that he just took Sophie and then left the country without warning?' Laura asked.

'That's right. Your mother was frantic with worry, and she did what she could to get Sophie back, but she and your father had disappeared without trace. We later found out that he changed his name. Then, shortly afterwards, you became ill with meningitis and were rushed into hospital.'

He paused and sighed heavily. 'I think you know the

rest. Your mother went home to get a change of clothes and as she drove back to the hospital she was involved in an accident. I think perhaps all the things that she had gone through—the stress of her marriage, then losing Sophie and your illness—helped to make her loss of memory more long-lasting than it otherwise might have been. I sometimes wonder if her mind just closed down after the accident, so that all the pain would be shut out.'

Laura said shakily, 'Did you ever find out what happened to my sister?'

Roger shook his head. 'We learned some things… It was a long time before your mother got her memory back, but when she met me we started to try to piece things together. We discovered that your father died in a skiing accident, and that Sophie was adopted by an English couple who were living abroad at the time.'

Nick interrupted, 'So it's possible that she could be traced?'

'I don't think so. We've tried. Emma left an address so that Laura or Sophie could contact her if they wanted to, but the adoption authorities won't allow a parent to contact the child once it has been adopted.'

'But surely, in the circumstances…' Laura put in. 'The way Sophie was taken, and the fact that now it's a life or death situation, surely the rules can be bent?'

'You mean because Sophie might be a possible bone-marrow donor?' Roger shook his head. 'I've already tried that. Emma won't hear of it. She says it's bad enough that Sophie must think she abandoned her, without trying to find her just so that she could be a donor. She won't do it.' He pressed his lips together. 'I went ahead and tried to find you both anyway, but I didn't have any success.'

He looked at Nick and Laura. 'I told you it wasn't a pleasant story.'

He got to his feet. 'I can show you some photographs, though, that were taken when the girls were little.' He smiled. 'For a long time Emma thought that they were pictures of Laura playing with a friend.'

It was strange for Laura, looking at pictures of herself as a child alongside the sister she hadn't known she had. She ran her finger over the outline of her sister's picture, as though that would bring her closer to her.

Nick said softly, 'Has this all been too much for you? You've had a lot of shocks to cope with just lately.'

'No, I'm all right,' she said huskily. 'In a way this has answered something that's always troubled me, always nagged away at the back of my mind.'

She looked up at him, glad that he was there to help her through it all, glad of his support. 'I've always had the feeling that something was missing in my life, but I thought it was down to the fact that I was adopted. I thought that if I found my mother, it would all come out right. Only it didn't, and now I think I know why. I think I must have always known in my subconscious that Sophie existed. She was my sister, my friend and my playmate, and then suddenly she disappeared from my life.'

'We'll look for her,' Nick said. 'We'll do whatever we can to find her.'

Laura nodded. 'Thank you for that.' It might be a fruitless search, but they would at least try to discover where Sophie had gone. Now that she knew that she had a sister, she wouldn't rest until she had found her.

Nick would be with her, and she trusted him. If it was at all possible, he would manage it, she was sure.

Until then, she felt as though her life was on hold once more.

CHAPTER NINE

'I'M NOT sure how to begin to look for Sophie,' Laura said distractedly. Her father's office was filled with sunlight that hurt her eyes, and she walked over to the window to adjust the blinds. Nick was with her in the office, and she knew that he was concerned for her. She just hoped that for now, at least, he and her father would try to curb their natural tendency to disagree.

'You said that Roger had tried everything,' her father said. 'I suppose that means he's gone through the usual routes of adoption agencies and the Salvation Army?'

'That's right. I don't know what to do. I'm desperate to find Sophie. Not just for myself, but for my mother. I wasn't able to be a marrow donor, but that doesn't mean that Sophie won't be a match.'

'Even if you find her,' Nick said, sounding a warning note, 'she might not agree to be a donor…just supposing it was possible, that is. I don't want you to get your hopes up, only to have them dashed.'

'I know… I know that it might not work out, but I have to try.'

Nick turned to David with a frown. 'Didn't you have any idea that Laura was a twin?'

Her father shook his head. 'None at all. You have to remember that when Laura was brought into hospital, her mother told us that she was separated from her husband. She wasn't able to get in touch with him, she had no idea where he was, and her thoughts were all centred on Laura at that time. Perhaps, if Emma hadn't been injured and lapsed into a coma, the whole story would have come out.'

He laid a hand on Laura's shoulder. 'I'm sorry. This must all be very distressing for you.'

'It's been difficult for me to take it all in,' she admitted. 'But I needed to know. There have always been questions at the back of my mind.'

'Things were very confused, you know, and a good deal of time went by before Emma recovered enough even to acknowledge the fact that she had a child. She had no memory of that, and her husband had still not been found. It was only years later that we learned that he had changed his name, and that he had lost his life some years before.'

Nick went and leaned on the edge of the desk, half sitting, his hand resting palm down on the polished wood. 'We should work together on this,' he said, looking directly at her father. 'We need to work out how we're going to set about finding Sophie.'

Her father nodded. 'Yes, you're right,' he said. 'I believe that many people try using the internet to find missing people these days. That might be worth looking into, especially since Sophie seems to have been out of the country for some time. She may still be out of the country, of course.'

Nick nodded thoughtfully. 'That's a good idea. We can get on with that right away. And there are the newspapers, too. They often have sections for relatives or friends searching for long lost people.'

Laura was doubtful. 'That would be a long shot, though, wouldn't it? I don't hold out much hope of that type of approach being successful.'

'But it's worth a try, don't you think?'

She nodded. 'Anything's worth a try.'

Her bleeper went off then, and she quickly checked it. 'I must get back to A and E,' she said. 'I'll have to come up with some other ways of getting in touch with Sophie, just in case the internet doesn't work out. Perhaps I'll give my friend in the records office a ring. I'll talk to you later, Dad.'

'All right, love.'

Nick straightened up and went to follow Laura, but David said quickly, 'Do you have a few minutes to spare, Nick?' Laura and Nick both turned around. 'This is about work and these wretched cost-cutting measures that we need to put in place, and all because of your single-minded ambition.' He glowered at him. 'You must have foreseen the extent of the damage these changes of yours were going to cause, but now I'm the one who's left trying to find ways to patch it up as best I can.'

'I don't follow that argument. These changes are for the good of the hospital, and you know it.'

'That's as maybe.' Her father's tone was tetchy. 'Anyway, I may have come up with a way to alleviate some of the expense. It occurred to me that when the outpatient departments close down in the evenings and at weekends, the facilities are being wasted. We could think about getting GPs to use them for their weekend emergency cover. They would benefit, and it would provide us with a source of income that we could use to offset some of the costs. What do you think?'

Nick nodded cautiously. 'That sounds good to me. We'll have to look into it.'

Laura didn't stop to hear any more, but it was clear to her that her father was very worried about impending job cuts. He was doing all that he could to avert redundancies, but would it be enough?

She hurried to A and E to find out what the emergency was.

'I need you to look at Mr Williams,' Sarah said, as soon as she walked into the department. 'He's complaining of a really severe headache, and he says that it came on very quickly. Since he's been here, he's been sick, and he looks to be on the verge of collapse.'

'OK, I'll go and examine him right away.'

Laura checked her patient over quickly. He was in a lot of pain and he wasn't very responsive to her gentle questioning.

'John,' she said quietly, 'I'm just going to take some blood from you so that we can do some tests. I'll give you something for the pain. Just lie still and try to relax.'

'His blood pressure's very high,' she told Sarah, a few moments later. 'I'm going to intubate him and put him on oxygen, and as soon as I've done that he needs to go for a CT scan. I'm rather worried about his changing neurological signs.'

While she waited for John to come back from his CT scan, she sent off blood to the lab and then went to check on other patients.

When he returned, she went straight to him and examined him once more. All at once he started to fit.

'Let's put an IV line in,' she told Sarah urgently. 'We'll give him diazepam to control the fit, and I want an arterial line so that we can measure his BP continually. Get Nick down here quickly, and see if you can get hold of a neurosurgeon. I'll notify Theatre to stand by.'

Nick was with her in a matter of minutes. 'How's he doing?'

'The CT scan shows what looks like a Berry aneurysm. It's ten millimetres in diameter and his blood pressure isn't helping. I think we need to get him to surgery straight away, before it ruptures—if it hasn't already started to leak.'

He nodded. 'His intracranial pressure is rising. We'll try and get that down with mannitol, and if he stays hypertensive, we'll have to consider bringing that down with sodium nitroprusside.' He shot her a quick glance. 'Have you sent for a neurosurgeon?'

'Mr Markham is on his way.'

'Good. The sooner he gets to surgery, the better. If the aneurysm ruptures, his chances will be grim.'

'I know. I hope he pulls through. He has two young children.' She winced. 'As soon as Mr Markham has examined him, I'll go and have a word with his wife.'

The neurosurgeon appeared as she was speaking. 'What are we dealing with here?'

Laura related the patient's history, while he checked him over. When he had finished, he said, 'Yes, it's definitely looks like a Berry aneurysm—congenital weakness of the blood vessel and the high blood pressure has caused it to distend. I'll take him into Theatre and clip it at the base.'

Laura went to find her patient's wife in the relatives' waiting room. 'Mr Markham will operate right away,' she told the woman. 'He will seal off the aneurysm with a magnetic clip to prevent it from bursting.'

'I didn't know what was happening to him,' Mrs Williams said, battling against the tears that were threatening to spill down over her cheeks. 'It all happened so suddenly, and now he's being operated on. One minute he was all right and now he's fighting for his life. I'm so frightened.'

'I know it's been a shock for you,' Laura said gently. 'The good thing is that we think we've caught it before it ruptured, and we're doing everything that we can to help him. As soon as I have any news I'll come and let you know.'

'Thank you.'

Laura went back to A and E, and found that Nick was battling to save a patient who had suffered a sudden heart attack.

She went to help him, and for the next half-hour they worked to stabilise the man's condition.

'I think he's out of danger now,' Nick said at last. 'Thanks, Laura. I'll get him transferred to the cardiac unit as soon as possible. Why don't you go and take a break? You've been working at full stretch all morning.'

'I think I will.'

She went outside to the quadrangle where everything was quiet, and the only sound was the drone of bees as they moved from flower to flower in the shrubbery.

Nick came and joined her there a few minutes later. 'I just spoke to Steve Markham. Your patient seems to have come through the surgery all right.'

Her eyes lit up and she made a brief smile. 'Oh, that's good news. At least something's going right.'

'You were the one who helped him to get through this. You were clear-thinking and you acted quickly to bring his blood pressure down. Most of all, you recognised the signs of an impending haemorrhage, and it's that, more than anything, that helped to save his life.'

'Well, I'm just thankful that it worked out. I wish I could do the same for my mother, but I feel so helpless. I don't know how to break out of this situation and make it better.'

He laid a hand on hers. 'Give it just a little longer before you start feeling low. We've time to search for your sister, and luck might turn out to be on our side. Your mother's a fighter...she pulled through a nasty accident all those years ago, and she worked her way back to health through long hours of physiotherapy and sheer willpower. Don't give up on her now. She'll go on struggling for her life with every ounce of strength she has, because now she has you to live for.'

Laura leaned closer to him, snuggling into the crook of his arm. 'You're such a lovely man,' she said huskily. 'How did I ever manage without you?'

'And you,' he returned unevenly, 'are beautiful...beautiful in spirit, heavenly to look at. I think I could go a little crazy over you.'

She chuckled. 'Only a little?'

'Are you laughing at me?' He swooped down on her and kissed her soundly, and where it was teasing at first, punishing her for her cheekiness, it suddenly became something infinitely more than that. His mouth moved on hers with passionate intensity, as though he wanted to drive everything from her mind but him.

She clung to him, breathless with excitement, his kisses bringing tingling sensation to flood through every part of her body.

All at once it was not enough that he simply kissed her. She wanted more, needed to be close to him, her heart aching for the sweet glide of his hands on her.

He lifted his head momentarily and they looked into each other's eyes. Wordlessly their lips met again, and his hands moved over her with delicious intimacy, exploring the softness of her breast and sweeping down to trace the smooth curve of her hip.

She gave herself up to the thrill of sensation that swirled in her head and sent the blood sizzling through her veins, but she came down to earth with a bump when she heard the sound of an ambulance siren in the distance.

Reluctantly, they drew apart, and Laura struggled to get her breathing under control. Her button-through top had come adrift from her skirt and she tucked it back in place with trembling hands.

'You've missed a button or two,' Nick said, his voice roughened, and she followed the direction of his gaze and felt the heat rush into her face.

She tidied herself up. 'I can't believe we just did that,' she whispered unsteadily. 'What was I thinking of?'

Nick grinned. 'Does it matter?'

'Of course it matters. We're at work, we're out here in the open—anyone could have come and found us. Besides…'

He raised a brow. 'Besides?'

This was all wrong, she thought, but she was too flustered to say what was on her mind. 'Stop teasing me, Nick. I can't think straight. I'm hot and bothered and I have to get back to work.'

She stood up and walked quickly away, needing to put some distance between them. What was the matter with her? She ought to be keeping Nick at arm's length, not reaching out to him as though her soul depended on him. It was no excuse to say that she had never felt like this before. He was a friend, a colleague, but she dared not get involved with him. It could turn out to be a disastrous relationship.

She went to the doctors' lounge, splashed her face with water at the basin and pulled in a few deep breaths before she felt in possession of herself enough to go and check on her patients.

Over the next few days she didn't know whether she was coming or going half the time. There was no let-up at work, and whenever she had any free time she made the journey to see her mother in hospital.

'How is she?' her father asked. He had been chatting with Sarah and Jenny, but now he came over to Laura and watched her write out forms for laboratory tests.

Laura shook her head. 'Not good.' Her emotions were very near the surface, and she daren't say any more for fear of giving herself away.

'I haven't had any luck with the internet search yet. Have you made any headway?'

'Not yet. Carol at the records office is doing her best, but she hasn't managed to come up with anything. I'm beginning to think that we're going to run out of time.'

He put an arm around her shoulder. 'Keep your chin up. They may even turn up a donor from the international list.'

'Yes, there's always that chance, I suppose.'

Nick approached the desk, and nodded to her father. 'Are you down here to check on the new emergency nurse scheme?'

David straightened up. 'It seems to be working out quite well, doesn't it? We're seeing a lot more patients going through A and E and the doctors are being freed up to deal with the more serious cases. I must say that I'm pleased with the way things are going.'

Nick was making an effort to get on with her father, but Laura thought there was still an element of guardedness between the two men.

'Me, too. Are you going to stay and watch things in action for a while?'

'I can't.' He looked down at his watch. 'I have to go for another interview with management in five minutes.'

'What's that about? Am I allowed to ask?'

David grimaced. 'I don't know myself yet. Time will tell.'

'I hope it goes all right for you.'

'Thanks.' He turned away and walked towards the door, and Laura saw him stiffen his shoulders. She frowned. He was putting on a brave front, but she guessed that something about this meeting was bothering him.

'Shall we go and get some lunch?' Nick suggested. 'I'm famished. It's been like bedlam in here for the last few hours and I'll be glad to get away for a while. I know a quiet little restaurant not far from here that does a good selection of food. What do you say?'

It wouldn't hurt to have lunch with him, would it? She was tired and hungry, and the thought of being able to relax for a while was tempting. 'It sounds good to me.' She sent the lab forms on their way and ran a hand through her hair. 'I ought to go and do something about this first.' Her bright curls had been tumbling around her eyes all morning.

'You look fine,' he said, smiling. 'You know very well that you can pull a comb through that lot, and it will be just as wild in five minutes' time. Come on, let's go.'

Nick's smile lit up his face and did strange melting things to her stomach. Her mouth twisted, but she went and grabbed her bag all the same and followed him out to the car park.

Over lunch, she told him about the search for her sister and the lack of news so far.

'Does your mother know what you're trying to do?'

'No. I know she was against the idea when Roger tried it, and even if she agreed to me having a go, I don't want to get her hopes up unnecessarily.'

'You've been going to see her a lot, lately, haven't you? It's a pity she lives so far away, and that I've been called in to work on my off-duty times just lately. I'll

be glad when we get another consultant on the team—
I've hardly seen you away from A and E.'

He sounded faintly aggrieved, and her heart missed a
beat. Had he wanted to see her? Her mind wandered to
the last time they had been alone together, and the way
he had kissed her.

Laura reached for her water glass and took a quick
gulp. 'I want to spend as much time as I can with her.
We've both had so little.'

'I know. This must be really hard for both of you.'

His fingers found hers across the table and a feeling
of warmth engulfed her. He was protective and sympa-
thetic and she realised how much she had come to rely
on him just lately. He had been there for her whenever
she had needed him, and now she looked into his eyes
and felt the bond between them so strongly that there
was no need for words.

They left the restaurant a while later and walked along
the path to the car. The sun was warm on their backs,
and Nick clasped her hand in his. Laura knew that, despite everything, she was falling in love with him.

Back at the hospital, Nick pointed out her father,
walking along the corridor towards his office.

'I wonder how his meeting went.'

Nick was frowning, and as Laura looked at her father
she felt suddenly afraid. He looked drained, as though
all the spirit had suddenly left him.

'Something's wrong,' she said. 'I must go and talk to
him.'

She was conscious of Nick by her side as she went
and laid a hand on her father's arm. He hadn't seen her,
but as she touched him he stopped walking and looked
at her as though he was in a daze.

'What happened?' she said. 'How did your meeting go?'

'Not too well.' He was trying to get a grip on himself, and Laura was worried.

Nick said quietly, 'Do you want to tell me what went on? Is it to do with the cost-cutting exercise?'

Her father stared at him, his features closed for a moment, but then he nodded briefly. They had reached his room by now, and he pushed open the door and they followed him in.

'I suppose, in a way, it was what I'd been expecting all along,' he told them. 'Even so, I must say it came as a bit of a shock. They told me they were sorry, but they didn't see any other way. They've had a lot of extra expenditure lately, and they need to put measures in place to balance their budget and they feel that the best way to do this to reorganise personnel and ultimately to downsize.'

He reached for a chair with a shaky hand and sat down. 'Losing someone in a high-salaried position is the most effective way to achieve their objectives, they say, and they tell me I have a choice to make. I can either take an early retirement package or accept redundancy.'

Laura watched as he seemed to slump in his chair. 'What did you tell them?'

'I told them that I didn't want either of those things. I'm not ready to retire, and I feel that I still have a lot to contribute to the smooth running of this hospital.'

He sent Nick a bitter glance. 'I've worked for years to put systems into place, working practices to ensure the successful running of departments, even though some of them are being overturned now. I don't see why I should be tossed aside, like an old shoe because they have to justify their budget spending.'

His jaw tightened. 'This is what comes of pushing for change. It never comes without a price, does it?'

Laura went and put her arm around his shoulders. 'I think it's a terrible way to treat you after all that you've done to make this hospital a better place. Have they forgotten all those hours you spent working to raise funds for the scanner? And what about the improved diagnostic measures you brought in when you were a consultant—don't they count for anything? They can't do this to you. There must be some way that you can fight it.'

'How? What with? It seems to me that they've made up their minds. They've given me until the end of next week to think things through.'

Laura shook her head and tried to think. Her father was holding on as best he could but, knowing him so well, she could guess at the pain he was going through right now. She had never seen him look as shaken as he did now.

'We'll think of something. There has to be a way.' He didn't deserve any of this. He was a wonderful man who saw the best in everyone and did what he could to help others through difficult times. He had found her when she'd been a vulnerable infant and had brought her back to health and cared for her as though she'd been his own child. She had never doubted his love for her. It was always there, and it was unconditional, and now it broke her heart to see him looking so low. How could this be happening to him now?

She looked across the room at Nick, and she could see that he was as concerned as she was.

'There must be other ways they can restructure their budget without losing key personnel,' he said. 'I never intended anything like this to happen. I wanted to do my best for the hospital, but this is the last thing I expected. Cost-cutting, streamlining working practices and ensuring that there's no waste of resources, yes, but not anything like this. You don't have to sit back and take it as if it was a done deal.'

Laura was sure that he meant what he said, but she couldn't see how they were going to change what looked to be inevitable.

His gaze meshed with hers over her father's slumped figure, and he must have read what was on her mind, because he frowned and said softly, 'Laura, we'll think of something.'

It hurt so badly to be caught in the middle of all this, torn between her love for Nick and her concern for her father.

Nick was like her father in a lot of ways. He cared deeply about people and he wanted to do his best for everyone, especially for the children in his care, and that was why he had made such an effort to push for modernisation. It was those qualities of compassion and determination that she saw in him that made her love for him grow and grow, but it was also those very ideals that were bringing about her father's downfall right now.

How could she love Nick and have a future with him and yet be loyal to her father at the same time? She owed her father so much. It was an impossible, unbearable situation to find herself in and she felt as though she was being ripped apart.

CHAPTER TEN

LAURA caught up with the doctor just as she had completed her rounds. 'Dr Hargreaves? I wondered if I could have a word with you about my mother. How is she today?'

Dr Hargreaves looked up from her case notes. 'Hello. You're Laura, aren't you? Emma talks about you a lot.' She smiled. 'Finding you after all this time has made her so happy.' She put the file down on the table by the nurses' station and said, 'Come into the office and we'll talk.'

Laura followed her into the small, neat room, and Dr Hargreaves waved her to a chair beside a large wooden desk. 'Can I get you a cup of coffee?'

Laura nodded. 'Thanks.'

The doctor went over to a filter machine and poured two cups, handing one of them to Laura. Then she sat down and faced her across the table.

'Your mother is seriously ill—but you know that, I'm sure. We've tried all the usual methods of treatment—chemotherapy, blood transfusions and so on—as you know. At the moment she's very tired, but she's free of infection, thank goodness, and we're nursing her in isolation in order to keep her that way.' She looked at Laura directly. 'If I may be frank with you...'

'Yes, please, that's what I want.'

'The truth is that we don't have a lot of time. We can support her in her fight against this illness, but if she's to survive, she needs a bone-marrow transplant, and she needs it quickly.'

'That's what I thought you would say.' Laura's expression was bleak.

They talked for a while longer, and Laura spent a little time with her mother, not wanting to tire her too much.

She drove back to the hospital with a heavy heart. She felt helpless. What could she do to keep her mother alive?

Nick wasn't on duty when she started her shift the next day, and as she looked around for him and discovered that he wasn't there, an ache started up deep within her chest.

She felt a sick sense of loss. What was she doing? The best thing would be to avoid him, to make sure that nothing could come of their relationship. How else was she going to convince herself that she was doing the right thing by her father?

These last few days, since her father's unhappy interview, she had felt as though she was caught on a stormy sea, being tossed in all directions. She wanted so much to support her father, but at the same time she missed Nick…oh, how she missed him. She yearned for his warmth and affection, the sound of his deep voice and laughing eyes.

'Nick's been involved in a series of meetings just lately,' Sarah told her. 'There was one yesterday while you were away, and there's another one this morning that's been going on for a couple of hours now. Something to do with the new minor injuries unit that's just been set up, I think. Your father's involved with that, isn't he?'

'He's making arrangements to employ some more

specialist nurses in the unit. There was a series of inter-views last week, and I think that's more or less sorted now.'

'We all feel terrible about what's happened to him, you know. We don't understand how this has all come about.'

Laura wasn't ready to explain what had been going on. As far as her colleagues were concerned it was a management decision, taken out of the blue as part of a restructuring exercise. They didn't know the part that Nick had played, in his push for modernisation.

'Your father is such a kind man,' Sarah was saying. 'He always has a cheerful word to say whenever he's down here, and he was such a good doctor when he worked with us in A and E. We missed him when he turned to administration, but at least he was still working in the hospital. I can't imagine the place without him.'

'That's how I feel. I've spoken to management about it, but they aren't really taking much notice of what I have to say. I'm his daughter, and they think I have a vested interest.'

'We ought to get together and protest. That might make them stop and think.'

Nick's dry tones cut in on them. 'Are you girls planning an uprising? You'd better take care...if you down tools the whole place will grind to a halt.'

'Now there's an idea...' Sarah pulled a face. 'Seriously, though, there ought to be something we can do.'

'I'm with you on that,' Nick murmured. 'I'm not convinced that a protest meeting will sway them, but if you think it's worth a try...at least you'll be expressing your support for David. They might just sit up and take notice.'

'I'll work something out. I'll have a word with the

others later this morning. Right now I must go and take a look at the latest arrivals.' She went off towards the waiting room, leaving Laura alone with Nick.

He moved closer to Laura and when she would have turned away, he touched her arm. 'Laura, let's go outside for a minute or two. I need to talk to you.'

'I need to get on,' she said evasively. 'I have to finish signing off these patients' notes.'

'They can wait for a few more minutes,' he said, taking hold of her and manoeuvring her towards the door. 'I've been trying to get you alone for the last couple of days, but we seem to keep missing each other.'

'Perhaps that's for the best.' Laura's voice was low, and she struggled to keep the shakiness out of it.

'Why do you say that?' His grey-blue eyes searched her face. 'You can't mean it.'

'I do.' They were outside by now, and the brilliance of the sun's rays dazzled her. She put a hand up to shield her eyes and was glad of the protection it afforded. Now he wouldn't be able to see her expression, to read the unhappiness in her face.

'You've been trying to avoid me, haven't you? Why, Laura? Why would you do that?'

'It doesn't feel right for me to be close to you. Not now, when my father is suffering because of you. You were the one who started all this, and I don't know what to do any more. I'm caught between the two of you. It feels as though I'm betraying his trust.'

Nick's hands circled her arms. 'I never meant to hurt him, Laura. Do you really believe that I would purposely do that?'

'No,' she said in a choked voice. 'I don't think you expected it to come to this…but you were always fighting with him over what you thought should happen, and management agreed with you. They weren't ever going to do all this work without trying to claw back some of their spending. Something had to give in the end. He's the one who's having to pay the price, and it isn't fair, don't you see that?'

'Of course I see that, but I didn't expect things to turn out this way. I never set out to harm him. Change and progress is all part of the ebb and flow, part of the way big institutions work, and how they eventually transform themselves into something else. Your father has been through this kind of change before. It isn't new to him, but I really didn't intend to make it a clash of personalities or cause him to lose his job.'

'But that's what's happening,' she insisted. 'It's hurting him, and ultimately he's suffering because of what you started, and I can't just go on being with you as if it didn't matter. I can't do that to him.'

'Laura, I love you, don't you know that? We need each other. Together we can be strong.'

The breath caught in her throat. He loved her. He had said it, declared it out loud, and her heart swelled with happiness, a warm tide of sensation flooding through her whole body.

His hands still circled her arms and she wanted more than anything to be able to return his love in equal measure, to have him fold her to him, to cherish her and keep her close.

But it would never work, would it, not if her father had been made to suffer because of him? She blinked back the tears that blurred her vision and shook her head.

'I love you, too, Nick,' she said in a soft, anguished voice, 'but I can't let it happen. The trouble with my father will always be there to spoil things between us. I'm sorry, but I need to be there for him right now. I know how badly this has hit him and I can't bear to see him so low. He's always stood by me. He's encouraged me when I've had doubts and he's given me strength when I was at a low ebb, and I have to stand by him now. I can't let him down. I can't let him think that none of this matters to me.'

It was breaking her heart to have to push him away, but she didn't see any other way out of this situation.

Nick's eyes were dark and intense as he searched her face. 'Do you really think your father would want you to be unhappy?'

'He has always told me to be true to myself, and in the end that's what I must be. I have to live with my conscience, and I don't think I can do that if I let you persuade me that none of this affects the two of us. It does…it ruins everything.'

She turned away from him, feeling utterly wretched. 'We can't be together, Nick. There's no future for us.' Her voice broke. 'I'm sorry. I wish that it could have been different.' She hurried away from him, before she lost control of herself altogether.

Back in A and E she tried to lose herself in her work. She examined a woman who had suffered a brief loss of consciousness some hours before, but who now appeared to have made a good recovery.

After looking at the results of tests, Laura told her, 'I believe you had what we call a transient ischaemic attack. It's nothing to worry about in itself, but as a preventative measure I'm going to prescribe a low dose of aspirin to be taken every day. I'm also going to refer you back to your GP for ongoing treatment to help regulate your blood fats and your high blood pressure.'

'Thank you, Doctor,' the woman said, looking relieved. 'I was really worried for a while. I thought I was having a stroke or something.'

'No, it wasn't a stroke. These things happen sometimes, and you can think of them as a warning, if you like.'

By the time her shift ended later that day, Laura was feeling bone weary. So many things were happening in her life and she didn't know how to handle any of them. If only there was a prescription for what ailed her.

'Laura, my love, you look tired to death.' Her father met up with her as she went to get her jacket from the doctors' lounge. 'Have you finished for the day?'

She nodded. 'And you? Are you coming home now? I thought we might have an evening together, if that's all right by you. I made pizza and salad earlier, and there's a bottle of wine in the fridge to wash it down. What do you think?'

He smiled. 'It sounds wonderful.' He walked along with her to the car park. 'There's something I need to tell you, though. I don't know how it will affect our plans...'

'Oh, what's that?'

'It's to do with a message I received earlier this afternoon. Someone from a local newspaper rang me and asked a few rather odd questions. It took me a while to understand what the man was saying, but then he explained that it was to do with something that Nick had set up. An advertisement, this man said.'

She looked at him, frowning. 'An advertisement? What kind of advertisement?'

'It was a missing person ad, apparently. Nick asked me for some photos a while back, photos of you mainly, though I think he also managed to get some of your mother—your natural mother—from her husband.

You've seen them, I think. They show her when she was in her twenties. Anyway, it turns out that without saying anything to anyone, he placed ads in papers here and in the counties around us in the hope that we might get to learn something of what might have happened to your sister.'

She stared at him. 'Nick did that? I know he said something about trying to search for her through the papers, but I didn't think anything would come of it. Have you spoken to him about it?'

'Yes, I had a word with him this afternoon. He was in a bit of a hurry, because he had another meeting to go to, but he did say that he hadn't wanted to tell us all the details of what was happening in case nothing came of it.'

'And the man on the phone, the man from the newspaper…what did he want?'

'He wanted to put us in touch with someone who may turn out to be Sophie. There are no guarantees, of course, but there's just a possibility that we may have found her. I've invited her round to the house this evening. Nick, too, since he started all this. He was the one who found her, so he should be here with us to help things go smoothly.'

'Oh…' Laura stumbled to a halt and placed a hand on her rib cage. Her heart was beating ten to the dozen, and for a moment she felt as though she was about to sway.

'Are you all right?' Her father put a hand to her elbow and looked at her in concern.

'Yes, I'm fine. It's such a shock. I hardly dared hope… Do you think it really might be her?'

'It's a strong possibility. From what the journalist was telling me, all the dates fit, and she did live abroad for a time. She has vague memories of being taken from her mother as a child, and that isn't something she read in the newspaper. Nick was very careful not to reveal details to her, but all this has come from the woman herself. Her father died when she was abroad, and some time after that she was adopted by a family who lived out there for a while. Eventually, they came back to the UK. Some years later, it turns out, she decided to come to Wales to start work as a nurse.'

Laura struggled to get her breath. 'Oh, Dad, can you imagine it? After all this time, to think that I might meet up with her again.' She looked at him, her eyes wide. 'I think I'm afraid. I don't know what to expect. What if it isn't her? What if it is, and she doesn't like me?'

He patted her hand. 'Let's just wait and see, shall we? We don't know anything for sure yet. And how can anyone not like you?'

Laura was still shaky when she arrived back at the house, but she gradually managed to calm herself down and prepare a meal, and braced herself for the meeting with their unexpected guest. When Nick arrived, she couldn't contain herself but flung her arms around him and hugged him close.

'Why didn't you tell me what you were up to? I never dreamed that we might get a result. I hoped and hoped, but nothing was happening, and now my sister might be coming here this very night. I can't take it all in.'

Laughing, he allowed her to pull him into the house, and he made no attempt to disentangle himself from her. Instead, he swooped down and kissed her until she was dizzy, and it was only when the doorbell rang and he reluctantly released her that she realised she had well and truly scotched her plans to keep her distance from him.

She stared up at him, uncertainty clouding her eyes. What would her father be thinking? She glanced around, but her father was in the kitchen, preparing coffee, and she relaxed a fraction.

'Perhaps you should answer the door,' Nick said quietly. He knew what she was thinking, but how could she make it right? Her father had asked him to come here, but that didn't mean he would be happy about their relationship, did it?

'Yes, of course.' She opened the door, and then gazed distractedly at the young woman who was standing outside, waiting patiently.

The girl had honey blonde curls and expressive green eyes, and a mouth that was gently curved in a hesitant smile. 'Hello,' she said. 'I'm Sophie. I've come to see Laura and Dr David Brett.'

'Good heavens,' Nick said, under his breath. 'It's amazing.' He was looking at Sophie as though he didn't believe his eyes.

Laura, too, was open mouthed with surprise. 'Sophie...' she whispered, after a moment. She clapped a hand to her mouth to still her trembling lips. 'You...must forgive me for staring at you like this, but you're the image of my mother when she was your age. It's incredible. You could almost be her twin.' She threw Nick a quick glance to see if he was thinking the same.

'We can show you the photos,' he told Sophie. 'The likeness is amazing.'

Sophie stood there, looking bemused, and Laura's father came to the door. 'Why are we keeping this young lady on the doorstep?' he chided gently.

He smiled at Sophie. 'Come in...come in, my dear. We all have a lot of catching up to do.'

*   *   *

Some hours later, Laura was still in a daze. After all these years she had found her sister, and it was all because of Nick. He had done this. Nick had made it all happen. She felt as though she was walking on air.

'You said my mother—our mother—is ill,' Sophie said quietly. 'I'd like to go and see her tomorrow, if that's all right. Do you think she'll be well enough to see me?'

'We'll take you to her,' Laura promised. 'She's being nursed in isolation at the moment to make sure that she's kept free from infection, but I know that she'll want to see you if it's at all possible.'

Sophie nodded. 'I'm a nurse, so I know all about the procedures. I'll ask the doctors to do the tests to find out if I can be a bone-marrow donor. The sooner we get started the better, from what I've heard.'

Laura hugged her. It was more than she had dared hope for. 'Bless you. Thank you for that, Sophie.'

'Will you stay here tonight?' her father asked. 'We can put you up in the guest room, if you like.'

'And I can give you a change of clothes,' Laura put in. 'We're about the same height and size.'

'Thanks. I'd like that. We've so much to talk about— I don't want to leave you now that I've found you after all this time.'

'I'll go and get the room ready for you.' Laura hurried upstairs, and when she came downstairs a short time later she looked around for Nick.

'He said he had to go,' her father told her. 'He asked me to say goodbye.'

Her spirits sank. He had gone without waiting to speak to her again, and now her stomach felt like lead.

'It doesn't matter. I'll probably see him at work on

Monday,' she mumbled. 'Unless he's involved in more meetings.'

'Yes, I expect so.' Her father looked at her oddly. He must be wondering why she was so taken aback.

She was desperately lonely without Nick. The weekend passed in a flurry of activity, but she was thinking about him throughout it all. She wanted to tell him about Sophie's blood test, about her hopes and fears, but he wasn't there with her and she only had herself to blame for that. What else could she have done?

Dr Hargreaves came to tell them about the results. 'We're in luck, girls. Sophie is a match. We can start to make plans for the transplant—if that's all right with you, Sophie?'

'Of course. I'll arrange for some time off work so that we can get on with it.'

'I'll do the same,' Laura said. 'I want to be with Sophie and my mother while this is going on. I'll book us into a hotel for a few days so that we have a base nearby.'

'Good.' Dr Hargreaves smiled. 'That's settled, then. We'll start your mother on a course of radiotherapy to destroy her abnormal marrow, and in the meantime we'll book the operating theatre for you, Sophie. We'll give you a general anaesthetic, and then we'll draw a small amount of bone marrow from your pelvic bone. You might be a bit sore for a couple of days afterwards, and a little tired, but you're fit and healthy, so it shouldn't be more than a week or so before you're back to normal.'

'I'm not worried about that,' Sophie said, 'just as long as this works, and my mother starts to get better. I haven't had time to even begin to get to know her, and I want that more than anything.'

'This is hard for you, I know,' Dr Hargreaves said in sympathy. 'After the radiation therapy your mother will be weak and prone to infection, so we have to be very careful. Give it time, though. At least we're in with a chance now.'

'I know.' Sophie pulled in a deep breath, as though she was psyching herself up for what was to come.

Laura gently squeezed her hand. 'We'll get through this, Sophie. You and me and Emma together.'

She looked at her sister with love and affection. Roger had talked about when she herself had been young and she had made up an imaginary friend as a comfort blanket, but perhaps she had been remembering her sister all along and wondering what had happened to her. 'This feels so right, you and me, finding each other again. It's as though things are back to how they should be.'

'That's exactly how I feel,' Sophie said with a smile. 'It's as though my life is complete again. I've found my family.'

A couple of days later, after the doctors had harvested Sophie's healthy bone marrow and processed it, they were ready to proceed with the transplant.

Laura and Sophie watched through a glass panel in an anteroom as Dr Hargreaves inserted a central venous catheter in a vein in their mother's neck to allow the bone marrow cells to be absorbed into her bloodstream. Their mother was lying back, supported by pillows, and she looked content with what was happening.

Laura went and phoned her father to keep him up to date with events. He was still at the hospital, but not in his office, and her call was put through to the reception desk, from where he was paged.

'How is your mother?' he asked, coming to take the call.

'She's having the transplant now,' she told him. 'So far, everything seems to be going to plan.' She paused, hearing a commotion on the other end of the line. 'How are things going your end? Have you heard any more from management? Is there any possibility that they will change their minds?'

He gave an odd sort of chuckle. 'I imagine that they're having to think things through. There have been a few confrontations around here just lately, and I think they've been taken by surprise.'

'How? What do you mean?' She frowned, hearing strange noises again, which seemed to be coming from where he was standing in Reception. 'What's going on back there? I can hear some really peculiar sounds.'

'Sarah and her colleagues are staging a protest. There's an amazing number of them. They're holding up placards and telling management that they have to think again. They say they don't want to see me go.'

Laura's mouth curved in a smile. 'That's wonderful. I'm glad that they're supporting you.'

He gave a soft laugh. 'It really surprised me, I can tell you. I didn't know that people cared enough. Apart from you, of course…and Nick. He was really angry when he found out what management were planning to do, and he went storming off to have a go at them. In fact, he's been having a go at them over the last week, day in, day out, never giving them a minute's peace. I've told him that he'd better stop or he'll be out on his ear, but you know Nick—he does his own thing.'

'I can't believe it. Why would he jeopardise his own position? After all, it was his push for changes that started the whole cost-cutting exercise, wasn't it?'

'Oh, I don't think he realised how many problems it would cause when he began all this. He did what he felt was in the best interests of the hospital, and you know, Laura, in a way he was right to go ahead. Everything has to move on. We need change in our lives or things would stagnate and we would never see any innovation or improvement.'

'I realise that, but you and Nick were always arguing and I thought you blamed him for what happened to you. When management took him up on the improvements he wanted, you were caught in the crossfire.'

'I was angry at first, I admit it. Everything I had worked for seemed to count for nothing, and it made me feel worthless for a time, but in reality Nick was just improving on what I had already put in place. As to management, they are always looking to streamline things, they're always worried about their budgets, and they sometimes try to take the easy way out by reducing the workforce. In truth, I don't think their decision was anything to do with Nick. It would have come about anyway.'

'But you were shocked. You weren't expecting it.'

'That's true. No one ever thinks it will happen to them, do they? But you mustn't think that I blame Nick any more. I don't. He's a fine young man—he's fiery and determined, and he's very clear-sighted. He knows what he wants and he goes out to get it, and I admire that in him. I don't always agree with him, mind, and that's why we argue, but argument can be a positive thing at times. It gets things out in the open, it clears the air, and then everyone knows where they stand.'

Laura struggled to take it all in. 'I've been worrying because I thought he had hurt you. I didn't know what to do.'

'You mustn't worry, love. Nick and I have mended our fences. We've talked it all through and we've agreed to put aside our differences.' She could almost feel him smiling at the other end of the line. 'Anyway,' he added, 'you have enough on your plate at the moment. You have your mother and your sister to worry about. Don't you concern yourself with what's going on here. I've a feeling that it's all going to turn out all right in the end.'

Laura wished that she could believe that. Had Nick really been supporting her father these last few days? Hope bubbled up inside her.

She rang off a few minutes later and went back to the anteroom. Roger was in there with Sophie, anxiously watching over his wife.

'I suppose there's nothing we can do but wait now,' he said.

Laura nodded. 'It will take some time for her body to begin producing blood cells from Sophie's, but we should have a clearer idea of how things are working out in a few weeks' time. The doctors will monitor her blood count regularly to see if the blood cells are increasing.'

Roger worried at his lower lip with his teeth. 'Do you think this will work? We've tried everything else. I don't think I could bear for things to go wrong now.'

He loved her mother very much, Laura could see that, and it made her happy to know it. 'We have to hope that it will turn out well, don't we?' she said quietly. 'I can't see any reason why things should go wrong. Sophie was a good match for her. The major problem will be that her immune system will be down for a while. We need to make sure that she's going to be kept free from infection while she's recovering.'

A nurse came and interrupted them. 'Emma's resting

now,' she said. 'She needs to sleep and recover her strength. Why don't you go home and come back tomorrow? We'll keep you informed if there are any major changes, but I think that's unlikely just yet.'

Roger shook his head. 'I'm going to stay here in case she wakes up. I want to be close at hand.' He turned to the girls. 'You go off and take a break. You've been here all day, and you need to go and have a change of scene.'

'Are you sure? Don't you want us to keep you company?' Sophie was concerned for him, but he shook his head.

'I'll be fine. I'm going to sit here and read my paper and keep an eye on things.'

'All right. You take care.' Sophie glanced at Laura. 'Shall we go back to the hotel and get something to eat?'

'That sounds like a good idea.'

'OK, then. To be honest, I could do with a rest myself. I feel really weary.'

'That's probably the effect of having some of your marrow removed. It was only a couple of days ago and you haven't taken time out to rest properly, have you? Let's go and get some supper and then you can have a lie-down.'

Back at the hotel, they shared a meal together and then Sophie went up to her room to catch up on some sleep.

Laura tried to phone Nick, anxious to hear his voice, wanting to explain to him that she had made a mistake in pushing him away, that she'd had it all wrong, but he wasn't answering his calls. Defeated, she left a message, telling him that she wanted to talk to him.

She sat out on the hotel's terrace, leaning back against an upholstered bench seat, feeling the warm evening air on her skin, while she looked out over the beautiful, landscaped gardens.

She was alone out there, and it would have been good to simply relax and absorb the tranquillity of the scene, but it was impossible. Inside, she was full of turmoil. Had she ruined everything with Nick? She wanted so much to see him, to be with him, and now there seemed to be very little chance of that. She had pushed him away and he wouldn't forgive her for that.

'How are things going?' The familiar deep voice smoothed over her like warm, dark chocolate.

She twisted around in her seat, looking up in startled wonder, to find Nick standing beside her. He looked wonderful, long and lean, square-jawed, a smile playing around his mouth, and her heart went into overdrive. 'Nick?'

'The woman at Reception told me that I might find you out here.' He came and sat down beside her. 'I didn't expect to find you all alone. Where's Sophie?'

'She's still tired after the operation. She's gone to her room to rest.'

He smiled. 'So I have you all to myself at last. Is it selfish of me to want that?'

'Is that what you want?' she asked softly.

'Oh, yes. It's what I've wanted more than anything for the last few weeks, but I didn't imagine that I would get anywhere. You were upset, angry with me, and I didn't dare hope that you would want to see me again.'

'I tried to call you. I left a message.'

'I know. I was on my way here and I didn't stop to answer my calls. I wanted to get here as soon as I could. I've missed you.'

'Have you?' Laura reached for his hand and laid hers over it, desperate to feel his warmth, to reassure herself that he was really there beside her and that she wasn't dreaming this. 'I wasn't angry with you. I was worried for my father's sake, and I didn't know what to do. I didn't want to hurt him.'

'I know. He told me what you said to him earlier today, and he's concerned about you. More than anything, he wants you to be happy.' He leaned forward and kissed her gently on the mouth, and her whole body quivered, her senses clamouring for more.

Nick's voice was thickened, low and husky. 'I love you, Laura. I want you to know that. This business with your father isn't a barrier to that. He and I have always argued, always exchanged banter. It's how we work together, how we get along. It doesn't mean that we don't like each other. We do. I respect him deeply. He was a marvellous doctor who taught me a lot, and now he's doing a good job as an administrator. But most of all he's looked after you and kept you safe and I'll always be grateful to him for that.'

She reached up and traced his jaw with her hand. 'I love you,' she said huskily. 'I don't think I deserve you, but you mean everything to me. I was lost and lonely without you.'

'That's never going to happen again, is it? We're going to see things through together. Emma…your father, we're going to be there for them.'

She nodded. 'I think Emma's going to pull through this. I have a feeling about it. But what's going to happen with my father? He said there was a protest. What's been going on?'

'People wanted to express their disgust at the way he had been treated. They made their point, and I believe that management has taken it on board.'

'And your meetings with them? My father said that

you had been trying to sort things out. What was that all about?'

'It's all done and dusted, I think. I showed them that the suggestions your father had made were going to make the various departments run smoothly and bolster their efficiency targets.'

'Did they agree with that?'

'They had to. There's no disputing the facts. Your father had already put forward the idea of the minor injuries unit to be run by specialist nurses. It will take some of the burden off the doctors in A and E, so that we'll be able to treat more patients, and there will be shorter waiting times. How can they afford to lose a key man who comes up with ideas that boost the hospital? And that's before we even get to the plan to allow GPs to use outpatient facilities for out-of-hours care. That will do a lot to help them balance the budget.'

'So...have they abandoned the idea of forcing him to accept early retirement or redundancy?'

He nodded. 'More than that, they've put it in writing. His contract is secure. There's no way they will call on him to leave before time.'

'Nick, I'm so happy.' She hugged him close, burying her head against his chest. 'I hardly dare believe that everything's working out for the best.'

'Believe it,' he said, bending his head to claim her lips once more. He kissed her tenderly. 'Anyway,' he murmured, 'they didn't take that much persuading. It was only one or two of the management team who were behaving in a blinkered fashion. The rest of them were open to discussion.'

'Thank you for doing all this for us, for helping my father, for finding Sophie. How will I ever manage without you?'

'You won't have to. I plan to keep you close by me, for ever and ever.' He folded her into his arms and kissed her until both of them had to come up for air.

He looked into her eyes and ran a finger lightly down her cheek. 'Will you marry me, Laura? Will you be my wife? I want you by my side for always.'

'Oh, yes. I will,' she whispered, kissing him feverishly once more. 'I love you so much.'

He held her close to him, kissing her on the forehead, her cheek, her lips. 'Perhaps we should get out of here and go somewhere more private,' he muttered unsteadily after a while. 'I could get carried away, having you so near.'

Breathlessly, she returned his gaze. 'Shall we go up to my room? No one will disturb us in there.'

He smiled. 'That's the best idea you've had all day.' He drew her into his arms once more, and kissed her with a passionate intensity that made her nerve endings sizzle. 'I love you, I need you…and I can't wait for you to be my wife.'

It was another two months before they felt it was the right time to get married. Two long months, Laura reflected as she looked around at the crowd of family and friends who were gathered at the reception to celebrate their wedding.

It had been worth the wait, though, to see her mother sitting by Roger's side, looking on fondly as Laura and Nick prepared to cut the cake. She was getting stronger every day.

Laura looked at her and wished that her adoptive mother could have been here, too, on this special day, but she felt a glow of reassurance inside, a knowledge that she would have given them her blessing.

Her father was poised with a camera in his hand, and her sister was there, too, laughing as Connor tried to creep away from his parents and get in on the picture.

It was a joyous, wonderful occasion, and as she looked into Nick's eyes and saw the love written there, Laura knew that they would be together for ever.

LIVE THE EMOTION

Modern Romance™
...seduction and
passion guaranteed

Tender Romance™
...love affairs that
last a lifetime

Medical Romance™
...medical drama
on the pulse

Historical Romance™
...rich, vivid and
passionate

Sensual Romance™
...sassy, sexy and
seductive

Blaze Romance™
...the temperature's
rising

27 new titles every month.

Live the emotion

MILLS & BOON®

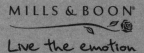

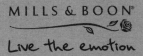

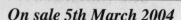

MILLS & BOON®

Live the emotion

The Elizabethan Season

A brand-new collection of sparkling historical romances

Volume 1 on sale from
5th March 2004

Available at most branches of WHSmith, Tesco, Martins, Borders, Eason, Sainsbury's and all good paperback bookshops.

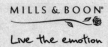

FREE!

4 Books
and a surprise gift!

We would like to take this opportunity to thank you for reading this Mills & Boon® book by offering you the chance to take FOUR more specially selected titles from the Medical Romance™ series absolutely FREE! We're also making this offer to introduce you to the benefits of the Reader Service™—

- ★ FREE home delivery
- ★ FREE gifts and competitions
- ★ FREE monthly Newsletter
- ★ Books available before they're in the shops
- ★ Exclusive Reader Service discount

Accepting these FREE books and gift places you under no obligation to buy; you may cancel at any time, even after receiving your free shipment. Simply complete your details below and return the entire page to the address below. *You don't even need a stamp!*

YES! Please send me 4 free Medical Romance books and a surprise gift. I understand that unless you hear from me, I will receive 6 superb new titles every month for just £2.60 each, postage and packing free. I am under no obligation to purchase any books and may cancel my subscription at any time. The free books and gift will be mine to keep in any case.

M4ZEE

Ms/Mrs/Miss/Mr ....Initials ....
BLOCK CAPITALS PLEASE

Surname ....

Address ....

....

....Postcode ....

Send this whole page to:
UK: The Reader Service, FREEPOST CN81, Croydon, CR9 3WZ
EIRE: The Reader Service, PO Box 4546, Kilcock, County Kildare (stamp required)

Offer not valid to current Reader Service subscribers to this series. We reserve the right to refuse an application and applicants must be aged 18 years or over. Only one application per household. Terms and prices subject to change without notice. Offer expires 30th May 2004. As a result of this application, you may receive offers from Harlequin Mills & Boon and other carefully selected companies. If you would prefer not to share in this opportunity please write to The Data Manager at the address above.

Mills & Boon® is a registered trademark owned by Harlequin Mills & Boon Limited.
Medical Romance™ is being used as a trademark.
The Reader Service™ is being used as a trademark.